LINDA HAYNER

ELLANOR'S EXCHANGE

Also by Linda Hayner
The Foundling

✦ A NOVEL ✦

Ellanor's Exchange

LINDA HAYNER

JOURNEY
FORTH™

Greenville, South Carolina

Library of Congress Cataloging-in-Publication Data

Hayner, Linda K.
   Ellanor's exchange / by Linda Hayner.
     p. cm.
   Summary: Ellanor, the teenaged daughter of a wealthy merchant, travels to London in the 1640s to find a titled husband but instead becomes enmeshed in the political struggles between Parliament and Charles I.
   ISBN 1-59166-462-4 (perfect bound pbk. : alk. paper)
   [1. Courtship—Fiction. 2. Spies—Fiction. 3. Courts and courtiers—Fiction. 4. Pym, John, 1584-1643—Fiction. 5. London (England)—Fiction. 6. Great Britain—History—Charles I, 1625-1649—Fiction.]
I. Title.
PZ7.H3149115Ell 2005
[E]—dc22

                            2005013011

Design by Jamie Miller
Cover Photos: © Digital Vision
Composition by Melissa Matos

ISBN 1-59166-462-4
15 14 13 12 11 10 9 8 7 6 5 4 3 2 1

FOR MY NIECE
Ella Sue

CONTENTS

Prologue	Spring 1640	1
One	Decision	5
Two	August 1640	9
Three	Leaving Home	13
Four	To Bath	19
Five	The Rose Garden	26
Six	Lord Wetherby and Lord Limbourne	32
Seven	To London	37
Eight	Beginnings	41
Nine	Lady Esancy	46
Ten	First Party	52
Eleven	Lord Netherfield's Library	58
Twelve	Derbyshire	66
Thirteen	Lucy Hay, Countess of Carlisle	78
Fourteen	Enter Roland	87
Fifteen	On Spying	94
Sixteen	Oatlands	97
Seventeen	Ladies	101
Eighteen	Threats	107
Nineteen	Confession	113
Twenty	Volunteers	123
Twenty-One	Searchers	133
Twenty-Two	The River	135
Twenty-Three	Warning	142
Twenty-Four	Outlaws	149
Twenty-Five	Rescue	157
Twenty-Six	Homecoming	162
Twenty-Seven	Friends	169
Twenty-Eight	Visitors	177
Twenty-Nine	Questions	184
Thirty	For Happiness	191

The riders galloped their horses over the spring grass. They skirted thorny thickets and flew over stone-filled ditches. They cleared the last hedgerow, green with new leaves, and pulled their mounts to a sliding stop in front of a man at the top of a low hill.

The girl jumped off her horse and ran to the man. "Father, he's the most wonderful horse in the world! Did you see him take the last fence?"

"Ellanor, it's a miracle you didn't break your neck." Master George Fitzhugh, gentleman, laughed. He gave his daughter a hug and then held a hand out to the second rider. "Good ride, Son, but I think she had you in the end."

"Did she? I think not." Paul shook his head.

"I did," said his sister.

Master Fitzhugh put his arm around his daughter's shoulders. "So, my girl, you like him, do you?"

"He's perfect. I'm going to call him Charlemagne."

"Charlemagne!" Paul made a face. "What an awful name for a horse."

"Well, dear brother, he bested your horse. Old Blacky there could hardly keep up."

"I'll have you know I had him under close rein all the way." Paul tugged a lock of his sister's red hair. "And, his name's Arthur, a good English name."

Master Fitzhugh pulled his children close to him. " 'Twas a grand sight, you two coming across the field neck and neck. Perhaps we shouldn't mention the fence jumping to your mother. Let's walk back so the horses can cool down."

Paul shivered in the evening air.

"Son?"

"Just a chill. Supper and a night's rest will put me right."

After eating only a bowl of soup, however, Paul took to his bed. "A bit tired," he said, "and a headache."

By morning Mistress Elizabeth Fitzhugh was certain that her eldest child and only son was ill of the influenza. Though many folk in the nearby towns of Bath and Wells had taken to their beds with the fever, she had hoped her family, living in the country, might be spared. She prayed silently as she bathed her son's face with cool cloths. She applied plasters to Paul's chest to ease his breathing and burned herbs to sweeten the air in his room.

Paul's cough worsened. He tossed on his bed and spoke fevered words none could understand.

Two days later Master and Mistress Fitzhugh buried their son. Only Mary Hartley, Baroness of Wilthrop, their neighbor to the north, walked with them behind the wagon that bore Paul's coffin. All others shuttered their homes and feared to walk out in the disease-stricken countryside.

At the grave site the vicar read the burial service. When he read, "Lord, Thou hast been our refuge, from one generation to another," Ellanor's father put his arm around her shoulders and pulled her to him. Mistress Fitzhugh cried quietly into her handkerchief and leaned on the arm of Lady Wilthrop.

Each of the mourners sprinkled a handful of soil onto the coffin. In the background the vicar continued, "Forasmuch as it hath pleased Almighty God, in His wise providence, to take out of this world the soul of our deceased Paul Fitzhugh, we therefore commit his body to the ground . . ."

Coaches arrived to take them home.

Master Fitzhugh kept his daughter close that spring. When he returned from business in the port city of Bristol, he and Ellanor rode out across Bishop's Manor. They spoke of matters important to the manor and surveyed a new pond that provided water for the sheep in an upper pasture. They heard petitions of the manor's tenants. One asked that the leaky roof of his cottage be fixed. Another requested permission to graze a second cow on the commons.

Late in June, father and daughter rode through a grove of ancient oak trees. Master Fitzhugh said, "It's been the joy of my life making these lands the best in the West Country. I haven't done badly for an old merchant."

Ellanor reined Charlemagne in and looked around. "I can't imagine a lovelier place in all of England."

Her father nodded. "Nor can I." He hesitated. "It will provide you with a worthy dowry."

Ellanor nodded. Any reminder that Paul would not share in this beauty saddened her.

"I have a bit of news," Master Fitzhugh continued.

Ellanor sat enjoying the warmth of the sun. "Hmmm?"

"Lady Wilthrop has offered to serve as your chaperone in London—"

Ellanor turned toward her father. Her jaw dropped open, and she didn't seem to be able to close it.

Master Fitzhugh chuckled. "I thought that would surprise you." He watched his daughter's face. "Say something, my dear."

"London?" Ellanor's voice squeaked. "I don't have to think a moment about going to London! What a frolic!"

Her father smiled. "It wouldn't be until the end of summer. I thought you might like a change of scenery." His voice trailed away.

"How thoughtless of me. I can't go on holiday, not so soon after . . . after . . ."

"Paul's death," her father finished for her.

"It doesn't seem right."

Her father's horse shifted under him, and he took some time bringing his mount alongside Charlemagne. "It's more than a holiday, Ellanor. You'll stay for the winter at least."

"A whole season in London?" This was beyond Ellanor's grandest dreams.

"You will learn the ways of the City and become a proper lady yourself. You know I've always wanted more for Paul, for you, for the name of Fitzhugh. I'm asking, my daughter, if you are willing to take up the task left unfinished by your brother."

Ellanor's smile faded to an expression of disbelief. "Me?"

Her father continued. "It's still possible for our family to gain a title by marriage." He reached out and took her hand. "You're a lovely girl and will marry well one day. Why not marry a nobleman?"

Ellanor pulled her hand from her father's. "I'm only fourteen."

"You've grown up so much this year. Besides, you wouldn't marry immediately, perhaps some months . . ." Master Fitzhugh's voice became pleading.

"Months?"

"A year, perhaps. And, you'd enjoy some time in London as well. Ellanor, please don't cry."

The fields of Bishop's Manor broke into flashes of green and gold as tears filled Ellanor's eyes. She turned away from her father. "That was for Paul, not for me."

"You are the family's hope. The opportunity is there. Lady Wilthrop has offered."

Ellanor turned away.

They rode home in silence.

CHAPTER ONE
DECISION

"Ellanor? You've not been riding with your father for over a week or said more than three words. Are you ill?" Mistress Fitzhugh tied a straw hat over her hair.

"No, I'm quite well, really." Ellanor did not look up from her book.

"Perhaps a walk will lift your spirits. I'd enjoy your company."

They walked through the front garden, past Mistress Fitzhugh's much-loved roses, then down a tree-shaded lane. Each walked in an earthen track worn by cart wheels. Between them grew tall grasses and weeds.

"Isn't this a lovely day?" asked Mistress Fitzhugh.

Ellanor nodded. She caught the stem of a flowering weed and pulled it free.

Mistress Fitzhugh led her daughter on for several more minutes before she spoke again. "We are far enough away from the house if you wish to speak. Only I will hear."

Ellanor stared hard at the small stones in the cart track. "There's nothing to say," she said.

At the end of the lane Mistress Fitzhugh led her daughter over a stile and into a horse pasture. She walked up a short hill to a large boulder and sat down. From here she could see the old manor house once owned by the Bishop of Bath and Wells. Smoke drifted from the chimneys, a reminder that the nights were still cool. She patted the bare rock next to her. "Come, Ellanor. Sit down."

Birds warbled and trilled. Insects hummed in the warm air. Leaves rustled softly.

Ellanor sat beside her mother. She studied the flower in her hand. "Mother, I don't want to be married."

"So your father spoke to you about going to London?"

Ellanor nodded. "Under the oak trees the day we rode to see the new pond."

"You don't want to go?"

Ellanor wiped some tears away on the back of her hand. "Part of me wants to go."

Her mother handed her a handkerchief. "But not all of you?"

Ellanor nodded and wiped her eyes with the handkerchief.

"What part of you wants to go?"

"Well, there's the palaces and the lords and ladies. Oh, and all the shops. I can't imagine what they must be like. And parties, I'd like the parties."

Mistress Fitzhugh nodded. "Yes, it's all quite grand. Your father and I visited the City some years ago. We had a wonderful time." Her mother shifted her seat so she could look out over the pastures behind the manor house. "Can you tell me what part of you doesn't want to go?"

Ellanor's sigh was long. "All I can think about is that father is sending me away to be married."

"That is a hard thought."

"It is," said Ellanor. Her shoulders sagged, and she bowed her head. "I feel as though he cares more about a title than about me."

Mistress Fitzhugh pulled her daughter close. "You are much more than a title to your father."

"It doesn't feel like it."

"When your father and I were young, we saved every farthing to invest in a voyage undertaken by a merchant from London. Heaven be thanked, he was an honest man, and the voyage was profitable. You were about five then. Remember when we spent an afternoon walking over the fields your father purchased with the profits?"

Ellanor nodded. "We ate under a big tree."

Mistress Fitzhugh nodded. "That was a wonderful day for your father. My wonderful days began when the men came to rethatch the roof, put new glazing in the windows, and fix the chimney. Seven years we lived with that leaky roof and wind whistling through cracked windows."

Ellanor nodded again.

"He did this all for his family."

"I know, but if Father wants a title, why doesn't he buy one? Why does he have to use me?"

"He could purchase a title, but he wants more than a baronetcy. And, my dear, your father isn't using you. I think he doesn't understand why you don't wish to serve our family as he has all his life."

Ellanor blew her nose. "I do want to help. I want to do what he asks, but how can I obey—"

"Ellanor, this isn't a matter of obedience. Your father has asked you, given you a choice. Something most young women never have."

"It's a horrible choice. If I stay here, Father will always be disappointed, and I'll know I'm the cause. If I go to London, Father will be happy, but I won't be."

"Why, my dear, you may enjoy living with Lady Wilthrop and learning all she has to teach you."

Ellanor gulped and took a shaky breath. "I don't want to be married."

A smile brushed Mistress Fitzhugh's lips. "You may change your mind one day."

"And I'll be gone so long. Father said I would be in London all winter."

Ellanor's Exchange

Mistress Fitzhugh sat quietly for some time before she answered. "You would leave Bishop's Manor for a year or two at least."

"A year or *two?*" Ellanor pulled back from her mother. She dropped the wilted flower and thought that she felt a lot like its bruised petals. "A year is a long time," she said.

"Yes, a very long time."

Ellanor stood and turned slowly to see all of Bishop's Manor she could. Her father's lands went as far as she could see.

"It's beautiful, isn't it?" Mistress Fitzhugh asked.

Ellanor said nothing.

"Someday," her mother spoke softly, "it will be yours, all of it."

Ellanor turned slowly to face her mother.

"With Paul gone . . ." Her mother's voice faded. "Yes, yours . . . to make of it what you will."

Ellanor climbed on the rock as if to see for the first time the only home she had known. Mine, she thought. Aloud she said, "It is beautiful." For the first time Ellanor realized that she was an important part of the future of the Fitzhugh family. I can do something that no one else, not even Father, can do. The thought surprised her. The flower lay forgotten. "Could I come home sometimes?" she asked her mother.

"You've decided, then?"

Ellanor jumped from the rock. "I'll go."

"And marriage?" asked her mother.

"Yes." Ellanor drew the word out. "But, not for one or *two* years at least."

Mistress Fitzhugh smiled and nodded. She pulled her daughter's hand through the crook of her elbow. "Let's go home and tidy ourselves before your father returns."

CHAPTER TWO

AUGUST 1640

"Well, my dear, it's time, isn't it?" Master Fitzhugh did not look up from his book.

"Ummm, yes." Mistress Fitzhugh poked a silk thread at the eye of her needle again. "Perhaps a bit earlier than I wish, all in all."

"The arrangements are far above what we might have hoped for."

"Of course. Such opportunity does not often come one's way." Mistress Fitzhugh pulled the green thread through the eye of the needle. "It was exceedingly gracious of Lady Wilthrop to offer."

"It's not as though we're acting above our place."

"Not at all." Mistress Fitzhugh put her needle to her embroidery.

"We must look to the future. We should attempt to improve our station." Her husband nodded emphatically.

"Indeed."

Master Fitzhugh marked his page with his finger. "I wonder what changed Ellanor's mind about going to London. You should have seen the look on her face when first I spoke to her."

"And, why not? Marriage is seldom a thought in the mind of a fourteen-year-old."

"She'll be fifteen come November."

Mistress Fitzhugh looked at her husband from under her eyebrows. "My dear." Her tone implied that her husband occasionally had wadding between his ears. "My dear, Ellanor changed her mind because she loves you, and she loves Bishop's Manor."

Master Fitzhugh cleared his throat twice before he said, "Oh, really."

"Yes, really."

"I've done it all for my children . . . for her. . . . She spoke with you, then?"

"With tears."

"And you said nothing to me?"

"What could I have said? Your proposal was quite a shock. She felt that you cared more about a title than about her happiness. She felt that you had put a . . . price, if you will, on your love for her."

"Oh."

Lady Fitzhugh went on. "You placed a heavy burden on her shoulders. She had to think it through. In the end, she decided to go."

"I didn't know . . . I just assumed—"

"That every girl sets her cap for a nobleman?"

"That every girl wants to visit London."

"We discussed that too. I think my descriptions of life in the City may have encouraged her decision in your favor."

"Bless you, my dear." Master Fitzhugh, still holding his book, rose from his chair to put a smacking kiss on his wife's cheek. He sat down again. "She's a good girl. I'm happy it's all settled."

Mistress Fitzhugh drew her needle through her embroidery. The green silk settled into the outline of an ivy leaf. "She will go. That's all that is settled."

"Perhaps she'll need a somewhat larger purse. Expenses will be great in London." Master Fitzhugh laid aside his book. He leaned forward, grabbed a poker, and prodded the dying fire. A smoldering log broke in two sending a shower of sparks up the chimney. "Jim! Where is that lad? Jim!"

A barefoot boy of about twelve ran into the room.

"Yes, sir. What was it you wanted, sir?"

Master Fitzhugh handed the poker to him. "Here. I've quite possibly ruined what was a fine fire. Don't know why I try. Lots of annoyance and very little heat, that's all I get. Ah, me." He settled back in his chair.

The young servant shifted the broken log and added another. In a few moments flames wrapped around the fresh log.

"Will that be all, sir?"

Mistress Fitzhugh dismissed him with a nod.

The Master moved his feet closer to the fire. "In for a penny, in for a pound, eh? When she goes, she must go as a lady. Our daughter at Court!"

"On the other side of the country, that's where she'll be. A long way from home." Mistress Fitzhugh guided another stitch into place. "Couldn't we find some nobleman's son here in the West Country?"

"We could, but I can't think of one who is worthy of Ellanor. Lady Wilthrop will do much better for her."

"Her daughter and two nieces made good matches," said Mistress Fitzhugh.

Master Fitzhugh turned to his wife. "You were just about Ellanor's age when we met."

"And you, my dear sir, were a most persistent suitor. My father nearly set his bailiff on you."

He chuckled. "We were too fast for old Peterson, weren't we?"

In the hallway Ellanor smiled at the thought of her father running from her grandfather's bailiff.

Mistress Fitzhugh looked up from her embroidery. "Ellanor? Is that you, dear? Do come in."

Ellanor curtsied to her parents. Then she crossed to her mother's chair and kneeled beside it.

"Do sit tonight, dear." Her mother motioned to the stool on which she'd had her feet. "Your father and I have been talking about your journey to London."

"You will, no doubt, soon overrun my letter of credit." Master Fitzhugh shook his head.

Ellanor looked up at her father. "I've been thinking. What if I don't find anyone?"

"Not find anyone?" Master Fitzhugh straightened in his chair. "Of course you will. There are dozens of noblemen without two coins to rub together. Poor estate management, I dare say. I don't see how you can't meet someone. And when they catch sight of you," he winked at his daughter, "each will have to take his place in a very long line."

"I don't know anybody in London."

"That's what Lady Wilthrop is for. She'll introduce you to all the people you'll need to know." Mistress Fitzhugh spoke as if she were repeating an earlier argument. "This will be a wonderful adventure for you, Ellanor, something I would love to have done. To be there with no ties, so to speak, with the world at your feet . . ."

"Anyway, it's too late to send a refusal to Lady Wilthrop," said her father.

CHAPTER THREE
LEAVING HOME

Lady Mary Hartley, Baroness of Wilthrop, arrived ten days later. She rode a gray palfrey. Behind her came four carts. The first was piled high with her own trunks and boxes. Another carried two maids and their boxes. The last two carts held everything else Lady Wilthrop thought she might need on her journey to London. Eight guards protected the little caravan from rogues and thieves.

Ellanor watched from her bedroom window. Her cat, Alfred, stretched and relaxed on the warm window sill. Ellanor stroked his long gray fur.

"You're getting fat!"

Alfred purred.

"After I leave, who will stroke you?" Ellanor worked her fingertips deep into Alfred's fur. Alfred raised his head to nudge her hand with his nose.

In the yard below, her parents greeted Lady Wilthrop. The four carts and their guards disappeared around a corner.

"Mistress Ellanor! Mistress?" Ellanor's maid hurried in and curtsied. "Your mother requires your presence in the large parlor."

Ellanor turned from the window. "Priscilla, did you see how much Lady Wilthrop is taking? Four carts. She has four carts loaded down. Could she possibly need all that?"

"No, I didn't see. I've been tidying the parlor for the fourth time today. Mrs. Trent doesn't care that I'm your maid and that I have lots to do—" Priscilla's disagreements with the Fitzhugh's housekeeper never ended. She stopped short and joined her mistress at the window. "Four carts? Where are they?"

"They've been taken to the barn. . . . Are you ready? Packed and everything?"

"Yes, Mistress. I've been ready forever."

"You wouldn't rather stay here? Won't you miss your family?"

Priscilla shook her head. "All my brothers and sisters—imagine being sorry to leave the six of them behind. Frances and Sally can hardly wait 'til I'm gone. They both want my bed in the loft. Mind you, there will be a fight over who has to do my work. Are you sad to go?"

"I don't know. First, I can hardly wait; then I don't want to leave. I can't wait to see London, but I know I don't want to get married." Ellanor scratched Alfred's chin.

"As long as we have lots of fun. Now, you must come down or I'll be scolded."

Ellanor entered the parlor and saw that her mother and Lady Wilthrop had seated themselves at a small table and were already deep in conversation.

The visitor greeted Ellanor with a nod. "You've grown up since my last visit."

Ellanor curtsied. "It's a pleasure to see you again Lady Wilthrop," she said and sat beside her mother. The tea was hot and the scones freshly baked. The women's conversation soon turned to the journey to London.

"I envy my daughter the opportunity you've given her." Mistress Fitzhugh smiled at her daughter over the rim of her tea cup.

"Much must be accomplished before Ellanor can enter society, let alone make a suitable marriage."

"You'll find Ellanor a willing pupil. She and we appreciate your condescension in extending this invitation."

Lady Wilthrop waved the compliment away. "Not at all. You recall that I made an advantageous marriage. It quite changed my husband's fortunes and gave my family an entrance at Court. A small entrance to be sure, but we used it well. Who knows what will become of Ellanor in London society?"

"Indeed." Mistress Fitzhugh spread clotted cream on a bite of scone. "I want Ellanor to be happy."

"Happy? Happy is doing one's duty to one's self and one's family. Ellanor will be well presented. You may trust me on that. I've introduced a daughter and two nieces. All made exceptional alliances, and I'll do my best for the name of Fitzhugh. When it becomes appropriate to make a decision regarding a match, there will be several worthy families from which to choose." Lady Wilthrop leaned toward her hostess. "I tell you now with every confidence that your family may look forward to an honorable alliance. Master Fitzhugh is well-known for his support of the protestant cause on the continent as well as for the success of his trading ventures." She sat back.

After a second cup of tea, Mistress Fitzhugh said, "If you wish, I'd like you to see Ellanor's traveling clothes." The women rose and Ellanor stood respectfully. "I hope they'll be satisfactory. We followed your advice to the letter." Mistress Fitzhugh's voice faded as she led Lady Wilthrop out of the parlor. Ellanor sat down again. She took the last scone, spooned on a layer of thick cream, and topped it with strawberry preserves. She licked the edges so nothing dribbled onto her plate.

She looked out of the parlor window. Cattle dotted a large enclosed pasture. On a farther hill, sheep grazed in long grass under the oak trees. Other fields, divided into strips as they had been for hundreds of years, were planted with wheat and oats, almost ready for harvest. It was easy to pick out the strips planted with maize. Her father was one of the first to plant this grain from the New World. At first, no one knew whether animals would eat it until, one morning, the steward found evidence that deer had been chewing on the tender ears.

This would have been Paul's inheritance, she thought.

"Miss?"

Ellanor jumped.

"Sorry to disturb you, Miss. May I clear away?"

The next morning a heavy thump awakened Ellanor. It was followed by a loud whisper. "Quiet. Want to disturb the lass?"

The instructions were followed by a crash. "Oi, what did you do that for?" said the voice. "Now, quit hoppin' about and grab your end of the trunk."

"I think I broke my finger," said a second voice.

"Well, holdin' it under your arm won't mend it. Put your back into it."

"I tell you—"

The first voice held no sympathy. "Help me shift this trunk, or I'll break another finger."

Low grumbles and whispered instructions were punctuated by fourteen thuds. Ellanor counted them. The two men let her trunk bounce down every step. She waited until their voices died away before she laughed out loud.

Mother will have an apoplexy, she thought. That's a new trunk. Well, no matter. It will bounce in the cart all the way to London. Ellanor sat up and swung her feet out of bed.

Priscilla arrived to hurry her mistress along.

Behind her, Albert stalked through the door. The fur down the center of his back stood straight up. His ears were flat against his head, and his tail switched back and forth.

"He's put out with all the bother." Priscilla laid out her mistress's riding habit. "He won't stay out of the way, so he gets the boot every time he turns around."

Ellanor joined her parents and Lady Wilthrop at the breakfast table. Cook had outdone herself. The toast was still warm when it reached the table, and her eggs and gammon were fried exactly as Ellanor liked them. In the background, members of the household moved about and called to each other. Once the men had finished carrying Lady Wilthrop's trunks and boxes out to the carts, the house became quiet. Only attempts at conversation around the table interrupted the silence.

From time to time Mistress Fitzhugh dabbed at her eyes with her handkerchief. She poured herself more tea and moved closer to her daughter.

Ellanor felt her mother's hand close over hers. A lump came to Ellanor's throat. It made swallowing her breakfast difficult.

Across the table Master Fitzhugh tried to discuss the details of the journey with Lady Wilthrop, but his gaze kept returning to rest on his daughter.

When Lady Wilthrop wiped her lips and laid her serviette aside, Master Fitzhugh stood to escort her to the courtyard. He pressed a second letter of credit into her hands saying, "If I can't be there to assure myself that all is well, at least I can provide so my Ellanor will want for nothing." Lady Wilthrop carefully tucked the paper into her pocket. Ellanor and her mother walked behind them arm in arm.

Master Fitzhugh excused himself from Lady Wilthrop and motioned to his wife and daughter to join him in the shade of an old chestnut tree. "My dear," he said to Ellanor, "my dearest daughter." He opened his arms and hugged Ellanor. After a moment he added Mistress Fitzhugh to the embrace. "Your mother and I will miss you terribly."

Mistress Fitzhugh stepped back and searched through her pockets for a dry handkerchief. "I'm missing you already, and you've not passed the gate."

Her father continued. "We're so proud of you. Thank you for taking up the task—my fondest dream—left by your brother. Rest his soul." He cleared his throat. "Remember your duty to Lady Wilthrop." He took a small package from his pocket. "A gift from your mother and me to remind you of home."

Ellanor tore the paper away. It was a pair of gray riding gloves. "They're so soft." She put them on at once.

Mistress Fitzhugh sniffed. "Do write, Ellanor. A letter will so brighten my day." She hugged Ellanor again.

They walked to the carts. Her father helped her mount and laid a hand on Charlemagne's neck. "A good horse, this," he said and dragged a large handkerchief from his coat pocket and blew his nose.

Ellanor looked around for Priscilla, who was still receiving instructions from her mother on how to behave. Priscilla's brothers and sisters were all shouting at once. "Send me something from London!" "Write to me!" "Send us presents!"

Priscilla gave her mother and father each a last hug and ran to join the caravan.

Lady Wilthrop gave the word. The outriders took their places, two in front and two behind the line of carts, and two on each side of the small column. Her ladyship led the train of riders and wagons from the courtyard.

Ellanor turned in her saddle and waved to the small group standing in front of the old manor house. Her mother's handkerchief fluttered in the morning sun. Her father raised his hand in farewell. Priscilla's parents waved while her brothers ran alongside the carts until they reached the stone bridge that marked the boundary of Bishop's Manor.

Ellanor felt that crossing the bridge somehow ended a part of her life. The thought caught her by surprise. I guess it's because I'll be gone for a long time, she thought. And, maybe, when I return, I'll be married. She shook that thought from her mind.

TO BATH

Lady Wilthrop spoke. "The time will pass quickly, Ellanor. You'll see them again before you know it."

Ellanor turned to Lady Wilthrop. She said, "I know," even though she felt that she didn't know at all.

Lady Wilthrop tried again. "It is difficult leaving your family, but I'm sure you'll enjoy London."

Ellanor frowned.

Lady Wilthrop went on. "I don't believe your father ever sent a ship out of Bristol with more love and care than he set you on the road this morning."

Ellanor bit her lower lip and studied a half-harvested field of grain. Men slowly moved forward swinging their scythes laying the stalks in neat rows. Women and children followed tying the grain in bundles. "He also expects to succeed," she said quietly.

"I think you need not worry on that point. We will do well by your family."

They rode silently for several minutes before Lady Wilthrop spoke again. "You do not wish to go to London?"

"I'm sure I will like London. Mother has told me about her time there with Father."

"Then you are concerned about marrying." Lady Wilthrop made the question into a statement to which Ellanor nodded. "As for that, you may relax for a while. It will hardly be part of our thinking for some time. The social season doesn't begin until the winter. Then, there's the matter of your wardrobe. That will keep several seamstresses busy for some weeks. Meanwhile, I will teach you the manners of the nobility."

Ellanor shook her head. "Mother says I've spent too much time with Father to ever learn proper manners."

"Running an estate does not mean one can shrug one's shoulders at good manners. I took over the Baron's affairs after his death and managed to remember how to be polite. If you apply yourself, I'm certain you will soon feel at ease."

"Yes, Lady Wilthrop." Ellanor sighed.

"Sit straight, Ellanor."

Ellanor straightened her back. She wasn't used to riding side-saddle. On the manor she always rode astride. Ellanor could tell Charlemagne wasn't used to it, either, by the way he kept trying to shift under her to balance her weight. She leaned forward and patted his neck. "A lot to learn for both of us," she said.

After another silence, Ellanor asked, "How far shall we ride today?"

"To Bath, my dear."

"How far is that?"

"I have no head for distance. We shall arrive in time for supper."

The road stretched before them. It wound past fields and through small villages. Ellanor looked down the road to a line of trees. The dark shadows under the trees offered cool shade from a morning made warm by the sun. When the caravan reached the trees, Ellanor realized they were entering a forest. The deep green shadows could hide dozens of outlaws. The guards held their pistols at the ready. Ellanor shivered and reined Charlemagne closer to Lady Wilthrop's horse.

"Have you ever been robbed, Lady Wilthrop?" Ellanor's voice was a whisper.

"You may speak up, child. The noise of the wagons has announced to everyone in the shire that we are here."

Ellanor wished the wheels of the carts had been better greased. She spoke a bit louder. "Have you ever been robbed?"

"The Baron was once. Horrid business it was. They took his money—he always carried too much, and I told him so—and his horse. Edward loved that horse. Strange to say, we found it a few days later in the small field behind the barn. The reins had been snapped. We never did find the thieves."

"Was Sir Edward injured?"

"A few bruises and a nasty blow to his pride." Lady Wilthrop leaned over and patted Ellanor's arm. "You are not to worry. I've taken every precaution."

After half an hour, the forest gave way to farmland. Ellanor felt as if she could breathe again.

The travelers rode to the only public house on the high street of a small village.

"You'd best be even more wary of the cutpurses in the village square on market day." Lady Wilthrop nodded toward the small collection of cottages and shops.

As soon as the caravan stopped, Ellanor stood in the stirrup to dismount.

"Ellanor! A proper lady waits for help to dismount." Lady Wilthrop was too late. One of the outriders jumped to Ellanor's side and caught her as she slid to the ground.

"That's right, Miss. Let me help you." He set her down lightly. "If you'll permit me, Miss, I'll tend to your horse." He took the reins from her fingers and led Charlemagne away.

Ellanor found Lady Wilthrop at her side. "We must work on your impetuous dismount."

"I always take care of Charlemagne myself. Father gave him to me."

"No longer." Lady Wilthrop took Ellanor's elbow and guided her to a bench under an oak tree. "You must remember that men and women of your station, and certainly of the noble classes, are above life's daily tasks. We have servants to do them for us, and happy they are to do so."

"That's not how it is at home."

"And it taught you responsibility. Now, your responsibilities change. You are a young lady of some standing in the country and will soon be at Court." Lady Wilthrop took a glass of cool cider from a serving maid. "This is what I will teach you, your responsibilities as a lady of standing." She tasted the cider. "Quite nice. And, Priscilla must learn the requirements of a lady's maid."

"Priscilla?" It had never occurred to Ellanor that Priscilla had anything to learn.

"Indeed."

"We're very good friends, you know."

"One must always have a friend to trust implicitly. However, a proper lady's maid must be trained in everything from the latest fashions and fabrics to . . . keeping one's hands well cared for." Lady Wilthrop held out her hands for a brief inspection. "I do hope she'll come along well."

Ellanor hoped so too. Being without Priscilla was not a happy thought.

For their midday stop, Lady Wilthrop led them to a fine inn. The innkeeper himself strode out to hold Lady Wilthrop's stirrup while she dismounted. He bowed over her hand and ushered her into the inn.

"Miss Ellanor?" The captain of the outriders waited to help her dismount.

"Oh! Sorry. I was watching the innkeeper. He's so very—"

The captain chuckled. "Yes, isn't he? His girth is ample testimony to his wife's ability in the kitchen. Now, down you come." He lifted Ellanor free of the saddle and set her down. "I'll escort you inside. I suggest that you join Lady Wilthrop in her chamber. You'll want to brush the dust from your clothes before your meal."

Ellanor patted her skirt. A small puff of dust flew up.

After their meal, Lady Wilthrop retired for a nap.

Ellanor found Priscilla sitting under a tree. She pulled her maid to her feet.

"Let's walk a little. Over there." She nodded toward a large pond. "Tell me what you've been doing all morning. Did you have dinner?"

"We ate out behind the kitchen."

The path followed the edge of the pond.

Ellanor pointed to a large carp. "What a meal he'd make! You'd not believe it. When I took a dish to serve myself, the innkeeper rushed in, snatched it away, and put a tiny portion on Lady Wilthrop's plate and a tinier bit on mine. If we'd not had five courses, I'd be starving!"

Priscilla took an apple from her pocket. "Want this?"

Ellanor grabbed the apple and bit in. "Thank you," she said around a large bite. "It's delicious." It cracked and crunched as she chewed. "The innkeeper must believe that ladies eat next to nothing. And afterwards, Lady Wilthrop scolded me for serving myself."

"I'm sure it's only in public, Mistress. Many's the time the staff of the Manor has commented on Lady Wilthrop's hearty appetite, especially for a mouthful of pheasant."

Ellanor tossed the apple core into the pond. The carp nudged it then sank out of sight.

That afternoon the countryside passed slowly. Lady Wilthrop would not let Ellanor walk even a short distance to rest her aching back. "Ladies," Lady Wilthrop said, "don't plod along leading their mounts. It looks common. It *is* common."

Ellanor studied her patroness. Her back hadn't bent an inch since they'd set out that morning. Ellanor passed some time by plaiting as much of Charlemagne's mane as she could reach. Pity I haven't any ribbons, she thought. They'd look quite cheerful. Then she took off her gloves and turned them inside out to see how they were stitched.

"Ellanor! A lady doesn't take off her gloves while riding."

Ellanor pulled the soft leather gloves back on. She wondered how Priscilla was getting on. Ellanor started to turn. Through her mind ran the phrase, "Ellanor, ladies don't—" She settled back in the saddle. Cows, sheep, stone walls, and small cottages provided no great interest. A lightning-blasted tree caught her eye. Its bare, black, twisted branches showed how terrible the stroke had been.

Finally, not caring whether ladies did or not, Ellanor turned around to see Priscilla. The maid had given up her seat in the cart and was walking alongside. She had picked a posy of wildflowers and tucked it in her shawl. She waved to Ellanor, who wondered if ladies ever waved back. She waved anyway and smiled, wishing she were walking, picking flowers, and chatting with her friend.

In the late afternoon they reached the town of Bath. The carts rattled past the cathedral, creaked their way up a long hill, and stopped in a small courtyard warm from the sun's reflection off gray stone walls. Around the door of the inn climbing roses, wall flowers, and pots of lavender scented the air. The pandemonium of noon repeated itself but in a more dignified manner. Ellanor remembered to wait for help dismounting.

"Miss? Would you step this way, please?"

Ellanor followed the boy through the broad front door and to her room.

"Oh, Mistress!" Priscilla waved her hands in the air. "Look. It's lovely, isn't it? The bed's so soft. My room's just through there." She pointed to a doorway in the corner. "We're living like queens, we are."

Ellanor sat on the bed. "The mattress must be filled with down."

Priscilla took a dress from Ellanor's trunk and removed the papers that kept it from creasing. Dried rose petals fluttered from the folds of material.

Ellanor opened a window. The cathedral sparkled like jewels in the green and gold valley below. "Priscilla, come see."

"Oh, it's lovely. And look below us, a rose garden. Your mum would love to see that when all the roses are in bloom."

"We must walk through it so I can write to her about it."

"Ellanor!" Lady Wilthrop's voice was followed immediately by a sharp rap on the door. "Are you ready to descend to the dining room?"

Priscilla jumped away from the window and opened the door.

"Not yet, Lady Wilthrop. I beg your pardon." Ellanor curtsied to her patroness.

Lady Wilthrop sat on a chair covered in a fine patterned silk. "Then, I shall oversee your preparations."

Barely fifteen minutes later, under Lady Wilthrop's brisk instructions, Ellanor stood ready.

"Well done, Priscilla. I had my doubts, but I see you'll do." Lady Wilthrop stood and closed her fan. "Ellanor, stand straight, tuck your chin a bit. . . . Good. Shoulders back. . . . Presentation is everything, everything. You represent your family, your name, as well as yourself." She examined her charge for a moment more. "Priscilla, we're ready. The door."

Ellanor was standing as tall as she could, her chin tucked and her shoulders back. She moved carefully across the room.

Lady Wilthrop sighed. "Like a willow, my girl, not a dead stick! I see we have much work to do."

THE ROSE GARDEN

That night it rained. Lady Wilthrop's personal maid, Martha, came early the next morning to tell Ellanor that her mistress would not leave Bath until the roads had dried. "This morning, her ladyship will take you on a walk about the town. Please join her at ten o'clock in the private parlor."

Ellanor and Priscilla arrived a few minutes early. A servant ushered them into the parlor fitted to serve the inn's best patrons. The ceiling beams were painted in patterns of flowers and leaves. A local craftsman had carved the countryside into the dark wood around the fireplace. Finches darted around oak leaves. Squirrels and rabbits hid under trailing vines. A fox crouched in one corner.

Lady Wilthrop and Martha soon joined them. "Gloves? Shawls? Come along then. There's much to see."

Bath Cathedral was much more beautiful than Ellanor had expected. The clerestory windows of clear glass allowed the sanctuary to be filled with light. It seemed that the ceiling floated high above the floor with no support at all.

Priscilla watched the people. Some entered the cathedral to sweep and dust, and some to pray. A man who, by his dress and bearing, was a nobleman didn't seem to care about the beauty around him. He walked slowly around the cathedral and yawned occasionally into a lace-edged handkerchief.

Almost under the cathedral were the ancient Roman baths. Though the hour was early, bathers already soaked in the warm mineral waters.

"Have you ever been in the pool?" Ellanor asked Lady Wilthrop.

"Once or twice. And I must confess it was most relaxing. I do not, of course, suffer from the complaints of advanced years." Lady Wilthrop swept her skirts over a puddle of water. "Have a care not to get your hems wet. This water leaves the most dreadful stains."

"It doesn't smell very nice either." Priscilla put her hand over her nose and mouth.

Ellanor put her handkerchief over her nose.

"Umm . . . Mistress?" Priscilla held Ellanor's elbow.

"What?"

"Over there. Oh, he's gone." Priscilla squinted into the shadows across the pool.

"Who?"

"A man, just there, by the second pillar."

Ellanor turned to look. "I don't see anyone."

"I saw him in the cathedral too."

"What was he doing?"

"Well, nothing really, walking around, yawning. But he kept looking at us."

"Oh, Priscilla!"

"Girls? Come along." Lady Wilthrop led them up a flight of stone stairs into a small room built around a fountain. They sat at a table overlooking the pool below. A server brought them glasses of mineral water from the fountain. Ellanor thought it tasted awful. After one sip Priscilla pushed her glass away. Lady Wilthrop finished her glass. "It's supposed to be quite beneficial, you know. But," she wrinkled her nose, "it is an acquired taste."

After lunch, Lady Wilthrop lay her serviette by her cup and saucer. "I must write some letters this afternoon. You are free to explore, but do not leave the inn and its gardens."

Within a few minutes, Ellanor and Priscilla entered the rose garden. The old gate swung shut behind them. The latch clicked softly. They followed first one path, then another. The warm air was heavy with the sweet smell of late summer roses. Bees bounced from blossom to blossom. In a shadowed corner a small fountain splashed. Soft green moss covered the wall behind it.

Ellanor held out her hand to catch some of the droplets. They sparkled on her hand and wrist. "This is perfect."

They found a low bench under a wooden arbor covered with climbing roses.

"It's so peaceful." Ellanor sat down.

Priscilla swatted at a bee. "If the bees will leave us alone."

A man stopped in front of the arbor. "Please forgive the intrusion," he said and bowed.

Priscilla whirled around. Ellanor jumped to her feet.

The man bowed a second time. "I didn't intend to startle you."

"We . . . I . . . didn't see you." Ellanor gathered her shawl around her shoulders. "We are just leaving." She took a step forward and then realized that the man blocked the pathway to the garden.

He didn't move aside but said, "Please don't leave. Permit me to introduce myself. I am Edmund Halsey, Viscount of Wetherby."

Ellanor curtsied. "We will take our leave, my lord."

Lord Wetherby didn't move. "I'm truly sorry to have startled you, Miss . . ."

"Ellanor Fitzhugh of Bishop's Manor."

"I was bored sitting in the inn and thought a turn in the garden would provide a diversion. When you passed by, I thought perhaps a bit of conversation . . . that is, it would please me if you were to take a glass of cider with me. The afternoon has grown quite warm. Yes, I'll see to it immediately." He turned and left the garden.

Ellanor said, "Oh, no, thank you, my lord," but she spoke to the air.

Priscilla stared after Lord Wetherby. "That's the man I saw this morning. He's following us!"

"What are you going on about?"

"Remember? When we were visiting the baths? I told you I'd seen a man at the cathedral. Every time we moved, so did he. Then at the baths he stood half-hidden by a pillar. That's him. That's the man."

"If he was hidden by a pillar—"

"Half-hidden—"

"All right then, half-hidden. How could you see him well enough to be sure?"

"I saw him well enough in the cathedral."

"Really, Priscilla. Why would a viscount, or anyone, watch us? You say that I have an imagination."

"Well, this makes three places I've seen him in one day." Priscilla tugged her mistress's sleeve. "Let's leave. We have no chaperone. Mistress!"

"He's already gone for the cider. I'll wait if only to be polite."

Priscilla went to the edge of the path to watch for the viscount. "Here he comes," she whispered. She returned to stand like a guard at the shoulder of her mistress.

Lord Wetherby reappeared, followed by two servants. One carried a tray with two glasses of cider and another carried a chair. Lord Wetherby settled into the chair. "Please sit down."

"Thank you, my lord." Ellanor sat on the bench and accepted the glass of cider.

He smiled. "Lovely, is it not?" He nodded his head in the direction of the garden. "I shall always remember my mother trying to persuade her roses to bloom into late summer."

"Yes, they are lovely. My mother also loves roses."

Lord Wetherby turned back to Ellanor. "You are visiting Bath with your family? Certainly not to take the waters."

"Oh, no. I've already tried the waters. They taste awful."

Lord Wetherby laughed. "I hope I never fall ill enough to have to drink them." He saluted her with his glass. "So, you must be on holiday."

"Yes, my lord."

"I hope you enjoy Bath, though there is little enough to do here."

"Actually, I'm on my way to London."

"Indeed? I, too, am on my way to London." He drank from his glass. "I don't believe I know your family, however. Fitzhugh, is it?"

"Yes, of Bishop's Manor."

Lord Wetherby knit his brows and shook his head.

"Near Wells."

"Ah, yes, Wells. I'm certain my family has some acquaintances in that area. It's been so long . . . the Wilthrops?"

"Lady Wilthrop?"

"Why, yes, of course. Lord Wilthrop and my late father, . . . now I recall. It is a small world as they say. You see, we are practically friends already."

Ellanor set her glass on the end of the bench. "Where is your home, my lord?"

The viscount shifted on his chair. "My family has estates in Devon. You'll be arriving in London soon?"

Ellanor leaned forward. "Have you ever been to Court?"

His lordship nodded. "Many times."

"I've read all the books my father has given me about the Court. Of course, a book can't tell one everything. What do you do there?"

"Nothing particular, really. I wait on His Majesty. And when did you say you will arrive in London?"

"I really couldn't say. You wait on King Charles? How do you serve him? Do you live at Court? It must be quite exciting."

"I see it's time to take my leave." Lord Wetherby put his half-empty glass on the ground beside his chair. Then he stood and bowed.

Ellanor rose. "How disappointing! Thank you for the cider. I shall tell Lady Wilthrop we've met."

"Please give me the pleasure of doing that. It'll be a surprise. I must be sure to greet the Baron before I leave Bath." Lord Wetherby bowed again. "It has been a pleasure." He followed a path between the rose beds and disappeared through the garden gate.

Ellanor turned to her maid. "He doesn't seem to know that Baron Wilthrop has died."

Priscilla let out a long breath. "I don't think he knows Lady Wilthrop at all."

"I wonder why he wanted to know when we would arrive in London. Perhaps he wanted to call on Lady Wilthrop. Oh well, we'll probably never see him again."

"I hope not."

"He was kind. You must admit he was kind."

"He didn't want to answer any of your questions about what he did at Court."

"He's nobility. They're different."

"I don't like him. And the least he could have done is move this great, heavy chair out of the way." Priscilla shoved the chair aside with difficulty, picked up their glasses, and went into the inn.

CHAPTER SIX

LORD WETHERBY AND LORD LIMBOURNE

The next morning Lord Wetherby watched Lady Wilthrop's caravan leave the inn. He stood well back from the window. When the last cart disappeared through the gate, he left his chamber, went down the back stairs, and stepped into the narrow lane at the back of the rose garden.

He pulled his hat brim down over his brow and gathered his cloak around him. He turned left and followed the lane until he reached a half-open gate. He slipped through and stood quietly until he was certain he was alone and unseen. The splash of fountains covered the sound of his footsteps as he crossed a small garden. At the back of a gray stone mansion, a door that looked as if it hadn't been opened in years swung inward at his touch. George had remembered to have the hinges oiled.

In the dark hallway Lord Wetherby paused for his eyes to become accustomed to the darkness. Then he moved quickly to the stairs. At the second floor another door opened to his touch. He stepped into the hall and walked quickly to the third door on his left. He rapped lightly before stepping into a large bed chamber.

"Were you seen?" George Satterthwaite, Earl of Limbourne kept his voice low.

The viscount laid his hat and cloak on a chair. "George," his voice was soft, "one does not engage in these weighty matters without taking care."

Lord Limbourne wrung his hands. "I suppose so, but I have no idea what my friends would say if they knew my callers were coming up back stairs in the manner of thieves." He walked over to a heavily-laden breakfast tray. "Have you eaten? I ordered a rather large breakfast, not knowing if you would sit down with me or no. I do hope the maid did not make comment to anyone."

Lord Wetherby studied his host. Even in his dressing gown Lord Limbourne looked rather like a large pear with arms, legs, and head. "I doubt the maid commented at all," he said. "However, I have already eaten."

Lord Limbourne waved his guest to a chair and sat down to his breakfast.

Lord Wetherby waited for him to finish a plate of gammon and eggs. Then he asked, "Have you thought any further on our discussion of last week?"

Lord Limbourne's empty spoon was poised over a bowl of flummery. "Indeed, I have." He lifted a spoonful of the creamy oatmeal mixture, looked it over carefully, then set it back in the bowl. "I need not tell you that this is somewhat outside my usual activity." He waved a hand when Lord Wetherby started to speak. "Don't misunderstand. I realize the importance of your request. We are discussing the security of the Crown, are we not? As long as you can assure me that what you ask is both necessary and entirely within the law, I am ready to serve my King."

"The King has enemies in his own house. What we do is absolutely necessary to discover who might be traitors to the throne."

"The risks—"

"Are not too great," Lord Wetherby finished for him. "And the King will reward his friends."

"Richly, I'm sure, but I hardly need treasure," said Lord Limbourne. He poured more cream on the flummery.

"Then serve for the love of your King. We must find the traitors and protect His Majesty." Lord Wetherby rested his elbows on the arms of the chair and put his fingertips together in the shape of a steeple. "I believe the greatest threat to the peace of the kingdom lies in the palace itself. Perhaps in the Queen's own chambers."

Lord Limbourne nodded his head. "I hear that the King tells Her Majesty everything. Not safe, I say. Not surprising that secrets do not remain secrets. Any woman, even a queen, will naturally tell all she knows. I suppose women have weaker minds; I'm sure I can't explain it beyond that."

"That's why we must place someone in the Queen's chambers. Someone to discover who does not keep the Queen's confidence."

Lord Limbourne pushed his tray away. "Many speak with Her Majesty every day."

"To be sure, but not all of them tattle to the radicals who challenge the authority of the Crown."

"I still find it difficult to believe that any of the Queen's own ladies in waiting would stoop to such behavior."

"I fear there is at least one who does." Lord Wetherby nodded. "Now, have you found a way to place our own eyes and ears in the Queen's household?"

"Perhaps. Lady Carlisle waits on the Queen every day. It is said she seldom allows anyone else to serve Her Majesty. She is looking for a personal companion."

"You know her well?"

Lord Limbourne shrugged. "I wouldn't say well. We see each other frequently during the winter season."

"You know her well enough to inform Her Ladyship of a worthy young girl who might serve as her companion?"

"Lady Carlisle will most likely approach her friends at Court. There's always a family wanting to put a daughter near the Queen."

Lord Wetherby leaned forward. "I believe I have found a girl I can use. You must help me get her into Lady Carlisle's household."

"Who is this girl?"

"You know Lady Wilthrop?"

Lord Limbourne jerked upright in his chair. "I know her well. You don't mean—"

"Exactly. She's bringing another girl to London. It would be quite an achievement for her to place the girl with Lady Carlisle, the Queen's closest confidant." Lord Wetherby sat back and laced his fingers across his waist.

"Were Lady Wilthrop ever to discover how you intend to use one of her young ladies . . ." Lord Limbourne brushed his hand across his brow. "She's a formidable woman."

"Oh, come now, my friend. You're doing her a great favor."

"So you say." Lord Limbourne chewed on a thumb nail. "What about the girl?"

"Does it matter? I've met her, a country girl from somewhere near Wells, I think she said. She seems to have no connections in London except Lady Wilthrop. She will be fortunate to have such an opportunity. If she actually helps me locate the traitor, she may even be rewarded."

"Can you depend on her?"

"She's young, simple, and like most girls her age, inquisitive. You should have heard the string of questions she put to me. I've little doubt but that within a matter of hours, she'll know more than all my spies have been able to discover in months. We'll soon know everything that goes on among the Queen's ladies."

"I doubt Lady Carlisle will want to take a young lady of unknown family."

Lord Wetherby smiled. "Really? With your connections, this should present no difficulty at all."

Lord Limbourne rested his chin on his chest and thought for a moment. "I'll be in London within the month. I'll speak to Lady Carlisle as soon as may be. No, perhaps I should speak directly to Lady Wilthrop. She can apply to Lady Carlisle, herself. Mind you, I can't guarantee that her ladyship will take the girl."

"For the sake of His Majesty's government, you must assure that she does." Lord Wetherby rose and swung his cloak over his shoulders. "We'll meet in London at the usual places. Make no effort to contact me otherwise." He closed the door softly behind him.

TO LONDON

Ellanor rode beside Lady Wilthrop as they left Bath. "Lady Wilthrop, did Lord Wetherby speak to you before we left Bath?" she asked. "He didn't want me to say anything to you because he wanted to surprise you."

"Lord Wetherby? Why, I've not seen him since . . . I can't remember. You've met him?"

"Yesterday he introduced himself to Priscilla and me. We were in the rose garden by the inn. It was so pretty with a fountain and all. Anyway, we sat under an arbor, and out of nowhere he appeared. He brought me a glass of cider and sat and talked."

"He introduced himself to you?"

"Yes. He said he knew you, so I thought it was all right . . . I guess. You see, we were alone with him. Unchaperoned. But we couldn't leave either. His chair blocked the path." As an afterthought she said, "Priscilla didn't like him at all."

Lady Wilthrop thought for a moment. "May I know what he said?"

"He wanted to know where I lived and who I was traveling with. I told you you were taking me to London."

"And that's all? I shouldn't worry."

CHAPTER 7: Ellanor's Exchange

Ellanor thought for a moment. "Then he said something odd. He said he'd speak to the Baron, meaning your husband."

"I am not aware that the Baron ever knew his lordship." Lady Wilthrop smiled at Ellanor. "He must have misspoken himself."

"Perhaps, but it sounded as though he knew you well."

"That is odd. And he said he would speak to me?"

Ellanor nodded.

"Perhaps we left too early for him."

That evening Ellanor and Priscilla sat close to the fireplace in their room.

"I asked Lady Wilthrop if Lord Wetherby greeted her."

"Did he?"

"No. She seemed surprised that I asked and wanted to know how I knew his lordship."

"Are we in trouble?" asked Priscilla.

"No, we're not in trouble."

"I don't like him."

"I told her that too."

Priscilla pulled her shawl around her shoulders. "It's cold away from the fire."

"It's the storm."

Raindrops fell down the chimney and sputtered in the flames. Priscilla got up and added a small log to the fire. "I hope we never see him again. He gives me the shivers," she said.

They sat and stared as the flames wrapped themselves around the logs. Ellanor curled her feet under her to keep them warm. Priscilla dragged a blanket out of a chest to wrap around herself.

"Wonder what he'll be like, your husband?" asked Priscilla.

Ellanor took a deep breath. "Lady Wilthrop says I needn't worry about that for some time. She said the season won't begin until the winter, and I need a new wardrobe. And," Ellanor grimaced, "I must learn better manners so I can meet my future husband."

"He'll have to be handsome, your husband, especially if he's poor. No bald head or bowed legs."

"I think his looks will not signify. It's the title that's important to Father." Ellanor's voice quavered. "Sometimes I want to gallop Charlemagne away down the road and never look back."

"You'd probably be married in two or three years even if you stayed home."

"In two or three years, to someone I knew, not a stranger." Ellanor brushed a tear away.

Priscilla moved closer and put her arm around Ellanor's shoulders. "You're not alone, Mistress. I'll stay by your side and help you all I can. Though how that might be, I don't know."

Four days later they reached Richmond where Lady Wilthrop hired a boat to travel down the Thames River to London. The carts and horses continued on the road.

The ebbing tide carried the boat along. All was quiet save for the occasional splash and gurgle of water on the boat's hull. Ellanor dabbled her fingers in the cool river water.

The shoreline passed by as if on a slow-moving stage. At the river's edge pairs of swans and their fleets of steely-gray cygnets drifted by. Smaller ducks paddled among the reeds. When they tipped up to feed from the river bottom, their tails bobbed in the current.

Green trees contrasted with golden fields of grain. Horses, cows, and geese grazed on a village's common land. Children sent to watch the animals sat in a circle under a tree; their voices carried across the water. One of the girls ran to pick some wild flowers. I'll bet they're making flower chains, thought Ellanor. She remembered her father's cows, flowers draped over their horns, heading home for the evening milking.

Farther on, cottages clustered around a parish church. Their whitewashed walls and buff-colored thatched roofs looked fresh and clean. A yellow hound ambled across the village square, his nose to the ground. He sniffed at a patch of bare earth warmed by the sun, lowered himself slowly, then stretched out. Ellanor could almost hear his sigh of lazy comfort.

Two boys with fishing poles waved. She and Priscilla waved back. Then the fishermen folded their hands behind their heads and settled back against the bank as though the effort of waving had exhausted them.

The river became noisier and busier as they neared Westminster. Boatloads of goods and animals for the city markets floated beside them. Ferries wove in and out carrying people from one side of the river to the other. Lady Wilthrop pointed out the buildings that were Westminster and the palace of Whitehall.

Then the journey was over. The oarsmen swung the boat toward the river bank and braced their oars against the current. The river churned around the boat, making the boards under Ellanor's feet vibrate. It felt as if the boat were straining to break free and run with the tide all the way to the North Sea.

The boat bumped against the landing. As soon as it was tied fast, Lady Wilthrop took the arm of one of her guards and led the girls up the steps. Waiting for them in the street above was Lady Wilthrop's coach. Ellanor and Priscilla spent a long time that evening wondering just how Lady Wilthrop's servants had known when she would arrive. It was several weeks later that Priscilla discovered that the coach and horses had been sent to the landing every day for a week to wait on the convenience of her ladyship and guests.

BEGINNINGS

When Lady Wilthrop considered herself fully recovered from her journey, she called Ellanor to her small sitting room.

"Ellanor, making your way among the nobility is hardly the same as moving about in the society of country gentry. Often it's a woman's social graces that first appeal to a suitor. Your deportment can charm those around you or, heaven forbid, embarrass them so they will never seek your company again. You must quickly unlearn old habits and learn many new ones. We shall begin at once."

Ellanor heard her patroness say "Ladies don't do . . ." so many times that she sometimes wondered if there were anything that ladies actually did. Lady Wilthrop called in her favorite seamstress, glover, lace maker, hosier, and shoemaker. Ellanor and Priscilla stood for hours to be fitted, pinned, and stitched. Hats, they learned, were out of fashion this year.

At the end of four weeks, Lady Wilthrop declared a short holiday. She watched Ellanor and Priscilla from her sitting room window. Somehow the girls had persuaded her most trusted servant, Fines, to take them riding. She turned to her visitor. "What do you think of my charge?"

Lord Limbourne joined her at the window. "Handles her horse well." He fancied himself a horseman.

"Are you still riding, then?" Lady Wilthrop eyed her guest's ample waist.

"No. No more. My back, you know. Not able to take exercise as I once did."

Lady Wilthrop's nod was polite. "Come, have some coffee. I see Hetty has left us everything we need." Lady Wilthrop poured equal amounts of hot milk and coffee into a cup. "You may like sugar. I'll let you decide."

Lord Limbourne appeared to roll across the room to the table. His elegantly cut clothes made him appear even rounder, though his tailor assured him that they made him look thinner.

"Tried this . . . this coffee just last week at a small coffee house on Lombard Street. How do you manage to keep a supply? I'm told it's very dear." He stirred in four spoonfuls of sugar before tasting the brew. "Not bad at all."

"A merchant in the City sees to my needs. He and my husband were friends." Lady Wilthrop poured herself a cup of coffee and sat down. "Now, Lord Limbourne, may I ask the reason for your visit this morning?"

"Please forgive me for calling on you at this hour and unan-nounced."

Lady Wilthrop nodded.

"I heard that you'd brought another young lady to London for the . . . ah . . . usual reason?"

"Indeed. Ellanor's family is landed and wealthy. Master Fitzhugh is an outstanding gentleman in the West Country."

"And it is time to marry into a title."

"Marriage is the easiest route. And I like to think I do two worthy families a service," she said.

Lord Limbourne nodded. "True. And may I say," he poked the air with his spoon, "this is the only nation in the world that provides such opportunity for its common folk, allowing country bumpkins to marry into noble families merely on the strength of their purses." He took a drink of his coffee.

"Allowing country bumpkins!" Lady Wilthrop's cup and saucer rattled in an unladylike way. "Allowing! I remind you my late husband married one of those country bumpkins and was exceedingly fortunate to have done so."

"I'm sure I meant no disrespect La—"

"Without my family hazarding its fortune, not to mention its eldest daughter—"

"And a beauty if I may say—"

"—on a poor baron whose lands were in such a state that highwaymen used them for hiding, and the house so derelict as to be near unlivable—"

"But, my lady, the title."

"What's a title, I demand to know, without the income to support it? My family rescued the sinking ship of Wilthrop, and grateful my late husband was."

"I'm sure he wa—"

"So do not refer to the favor shown us poor common folk—"

"Believe me, madam, I would never think of you as common—"

"And so you should not. It is the wealth of the merchant class that is the strength of the realm!"

Lord Limbourne puffed out his pink cheeks. He carried his coffee to the window. Outside the front gates of the Wilthrop mansion the Strand was alive with hurrying servants, students, apprentices, and tradespeople. How does she do it? he asked himself. Whenever I speak with her, she manages to wrong-foot me. And, here, when I've an especially important errand, she's done it again. He drank the last of his coffee.

"May I assume that you did not stir yourself so early in the morning without some worthy reason—other than arguing about my heritage?"

Lord Limbourne turned around. "My lady, you know I hold you in the highest regard. Forgive my thoughtless comments, I beg." He left the window and took a seat.

Lady Wilthrop's upper lip twitched only slightly. Lord Limbourne's family held several estates in East Anglia. He had become a frequent visitor shortly after the Baron's death. Lady Wilthrop was certain he wished to press a suit of marriage and add the Wilthrop estates and fortune to his own. The effort to be polite was becoming burdensome.

"I have knowledge of a magnificent opportunity. Learned of it a fortnight ago. Private party, you know."

"Yes?"

"Lady Carlisle has a place for a young lady in her household. I thought immediately of you and your young lady, that is, if you were chaperoning a young lady into society this season. I assumed . . . I know how generous you've been in past years, and I knew you'd want to hear of this." Lord Limbourne spread his hands wide. "Is it not a wonderful opportunity?"

"You're thinking of my current charge?"

"Possibly. Yes, why not?"

Lady Wilthrop nearly snorted. "Really! Do you suppose a woman of Lady Carlisle's family and influence needs to rely on, as you say, a 'country bumpkin' for companionship?"

"I believe, according to Lord We—. . . ah, according to my friends, this place might go to an English girl of good family. You see, Lady Carlisle has served the Queen for quite some months now and has little in common with the Queen's ladies of the chamber. French, you know. She has expressed a desire for an English companion."

Lady Wilthrop's guest perched on the edge of his chair. He seemed to quiver with excitement. "Your young lady's presence at Court will enlarge her prospects of marriage."

"Ellanor still has much to learn. She could not take such a position for some weeks, perhaps months."

"So long? Hmmm. I point out that she will meet many more noblemen in need of, to put it bluntly, lawful English money."

Lady Wilthrop took a sip of coffee and eyed him over the rim of her cup. "What you say is true, Lord Limbourne." She set her cup and saucer aside. "However, Ellanor is far from prepared for service at Court."

"Not at Court, precisely, but as a member of Lady Carlisle's household."

Lady Wilthrop thought for a moment. "I serve as Ellanor's chaperone, a duty not to be taken lightly given the confusion of these times. I could not fulfill that obligation if Ellanor were living in another household."

"Surely Lady Carlisle will serve in your place—"

"Really, my lord! That is presuming altogether too much on her ladyship."

Lord Limbourne shook his head. "But, madam, she has herself expressed this desire."

"Since you are so sure of her wishes, I shall contact Lady Carlisle."

"You'll contact her? Well, that will suit, I'm sure. And the sooner the better, we say."

"We?"

"Mere figure of speech. *I say*, yes, I say." Lord Limbourne rose and paced to the window and back again still carrying his empty cup and saucer.

"Lord Limbourne, you're quite distracted. Are you ill?"

"Dear me, no, but I must bid you good day."

Lady Wilthrop rang for her guest's cloak and hat. As soon as the parlor door closed behind him, she sat at a small desk and wrote a brief note to her friend, Lucy Hay, Countess of Carlisle.

CHAPTER NINE

LACY ESANCY

On the afternoon of November 24, Lady Wilthrop invited guests in for light refreshments. Mothers and daughters, eager for the winter's social season to begin, came to meet Ellanor. By the end of the afternoon, most agreed that Mistress Fitzhugh put herself forward well and had a pleasant manner, though she really must work on her west-country manner of speech.

Ellanor spent the afternoon comparing herself with her guests. They are so perfect, Ellanor thought. Look at Margaret Darcy, just a year older than I. She never spilled her tea even when Lady Newnham bumped her elbow. Ellanor looked down at her lap where she was hiding biscuit crumbs in the folds of her skirt.

"Mistress Ellanor, isn't it?"

Ellanor set her cup of tea on a small table and stood in the older lady's presence. She stepped so her skirts covered the crumbs that fell to the floor. "Good afternoon, Lady Greystone."

"No, no, my dear. I'll join you on the couch." Lady Greystone lowered herself with care. "I was wondering just where your family's estates were."

"Between Bath and Wells, my lady, though closer to Wells."

"I thought so. My husband Cecil, that is, Lord Greystone, and I toured in that area some years ago. Beautiful country. And isn't Wells lovely?"

Ellanor nodded and opened her mouth to answer, but Lady Greystone never paused. Ellanor caught references to Wells cathedral and the Bishop's palace.

"And the swans on the moat." Lady Greystone went on. "Do you know that they are trained to pull a bell cord when they wish to be fed? It's quite charming, really."

Ellanor smiled. This is the easiest conversation I've had yet, she thought. Nod at the right moment, appear interested, and don't yawn. Why did I think of that? She clenched her teeth and took a deep breath.

Ellanor only half heard as Lady Greystone continued, ". . . on our way to Bath. We both take the waters . . . always visit some new place . . . Wookey Hole . . . Witch of Wookey. You've heard of her?"

Ellanor smiled again. Everyone in the countryside knew of the Witch of Wookey. When someone finally had enough courage to enter her cave, they found the bones of an old woman and the goats she'd kept.

"Of course, I don't credit it with an ounce of truth, do you?" Lady Greystone tapped Ellanor's arm. "Do you?"

Ellanor jumped.

"Leave the poor child alone, Barbara." Lady Esancy waved Lady Greystone away. "She'll have nightmares with all of your tales. Besides, I'd like a moment with Lady Wilthrop's honored guest."

Ellanor rose to greet the elderly Catherine Poole, Countess of Esancy.

"Sit down, my dear. Take a deep breath and enjoy your tea, though it must be cold by now. Just a moment—Margaret! Yes, you, my dear. Please bring Mistress Ellanor another cup of tea."

Mistress Margaret Darcy had no choice but to obey.

"There you are." Lady Esancy handed the cup to Ellanor. "It was time someone rescued you. Lady Greystone does carry on." She nibbled on a biscuit until Ellanor finished most of her tea.

"I've been looking forward to meeting you. I don't make many calls when the weather turns cold, but the baroness is a dear friend, and I was eager to see her again. Also, I confess, I was eager to meet you."

Ellanor put her second cup by the first on the small table. "I know that Lady Wilthrop appreciates your presence. I was certain no one would come out in this weather. I have not ridden out for above three days." Ellanor laughed. "I'm sure Fines is happy about that."

"Fines takes you riding, does he?"

"Yes, though I believe he goes because Lady Wilthrop tells him he must. She does not care to ride when it is cold, and I must have a chaperone." Ellanor looked around the room. "I am surprised to see how many have come."

"We are all curious, my dear." Lady Esancy smiled. "Perhaps you'll someday be a member of one of our families."

Ellanor felt her face go as red as the carpet on the floor.

"I am old and take liberties. Forgive me. However, I feel it is always good to describe matters exactly as they are." Lady Esancy reached over and took Ellanor's hand. "You see, I have a grand nephew I would like you to meet. He is a fine young man in need of a wife."

"My father wishes me to marry a nobleman."

"Indeed. My nephew is of a noble family, my brother's grandson. And, as I say, he should be married."

"I don't know what to say. Lady Wilthrop oversees all of my engagements."

"If John knew that I was making matches behind his back, he'd be as red as you are." Lady Esancy smiled. "I'll speak to Lady Wilthrop, and all will be done as it should be. Rest assured, my nephew demands the social proprieties. He may be poor, but he remains a gentleman. I'll say no more. However, Mistress Ellanor, I hope we shall be friends regardless of how my plans . . . and yours . . . may develop."

Lady Esancy stood and brushed the biscuit crumbs from the folds of her skirt. "I can't eat biscuits without leaving a trail of crumbs." Her eyes twinkled. "It's a hazard of these afternoon gatherings."

After their guests had gone, Lady Wilthrop and Ellanor settled themselves in Lady Wilthrop's parlor. "You did well this afternoon. I'm quite sure you made a favorable impression."

Ellanor moaned. "I'm exhausted. My face is tired from smiling! My head is swimming with names and titles. I had no idea that finding a husband would be so tiring."

"It is a long process. You must meet all the best families."

"All? Even if they don't have sons?"

"Quite. You see, your name will be part of future conversations. What they say will do more to make your reputation than almost anything else."

"They don't want me; they want Father's money."

"Certainly they will speak of that." Lady Wilthrop sat back. "It is your father's fortune that enables you to set your sights quite high."

"I could marry the son of a merchant and be happy. Especially if he were like Father."

"Your parents want better for you and their grandchildren. You must not disappoint them."

"They'd understand if I told them I'd rather not."

"But you won't. We all must do many things we'd rather not. Marriage is frequently one of them."

"What if we don't love each other?"

"That's not expected. How could it be? Marriages in which large sums of money and land are involved are business agreements, not love matches. You will make of your marriage what you can. Love after marriage, while unusual, is not unheard of. Consider the Baron and me. In the beginning our marriage was a business contract, nothing more. His family needed my family's money, and my family wanted a title. However, with some effort, the Baron and I developed a warm regard each for the other."

The story of Lady Wilthrop's happy marriage didn't cheer Ellanor.

Later that evening Priscilla joined Ellanor in front of the fire. "I stayed in the kitchen the whole afternoon. All the servants went there. They all wanted to know about you."

"Did they?" Ellanor yawned.

"They're curious. After all, you might one day be their mistress. By the way, did you meet any man you liked?"

"No. I hardly had time to do more than curtsy a greeting before they excused themselves. Then it was on to light refreshments."

"What were they like?"

"Oh, small cakes and—"

Priscilla giggled. "No, the men."

"Oh. Quite old, actually. Some in their twenties, at least. But I didn't see them again until they called to escort their mothers and sisters home. Men," she emphasized the word, "evidently aren't fond of light refreshments."

"Maybe they didn't want to be around women who are planning their futures."

"I hadn't thought of that. It must not be so nice for them either." Ellanor curled her legs under her. "I met a lovely elderly lady, Lady Esancy. She was ever so kind, and she thinks her grand nephew needs a wife."

"Not one of the servants had an unkind word to say about her."

"You do gossip a lot, don't you?"

"Ummmm."

The girls stared into the fire for a few moments.

"Do you realize," Ellanor asked, "that I haven't yet gone to a proper party?"

"You probably haven't learned enough manners for a party."

"Thank you, Lady Priscilla."

In her parlor, Lady Wilthrop sat with her daybook open on her lap. The heavy blue velvet draperies moved gently in the cold drafts that crept in around the windows. The walls, covered with a silvery watered silk, shimmered in the firelight. The gold satin cushions of the chairs reflected the fire's warmth. A carpet of a deep blue and red pattern covered the floor in front of her chair.

Lady Wilthrop smiled and nodded. When Lady Esancy spoke with Ellanor, she thought, and actually sat beside her today, I nearly fell over. With that connection Ellanor could move her family higher than her father ever dreamed. Lady Wilthrop reread the invitation in her hand. She's made a good beginning. I hope Ellanor will be as fortunate as I was.

Lady Wilthrop's gaze rested on a miniature portrait of her husband. He had thought her foolish to pay good money for such a small likeness, but she had insisted. Lady Wilthrop kissed her finger and touched it to the picture. "My love, I must leave you now. It's late, and I must go to bed."

CHAPTER TEN

FIRST PARTY

Lady Wilthrop's coach stopped outside the Earl of Somerset's mansion. Hundreds of candles blazed inside and out. Footmen escorted her ladyship and Ellanor up the broad, curving stairway to the great hall where, for the first time, Ellanor heard herself announced, "Lady Mary Hartley, Baroness of Wilthrop, and Miss Ellanor Fitzhugh."

Ellanor felt her chin lift higher and her back go straighter. She gave her finest curtsy to the Earl of Somerset, who acknowledged them with a slight bow. "I hope we'll meet frequently this winter."

To Ellanor's surprise, he winked.

"Don't mind his lordship," Lady Wilthrop said after they left their host. "He winks at all the ladies and most likely winks at his reflection in the looking glass every morning."

A polite clearing of the throat caused them to turn. Bowing before them was a handsomely dressed man.

"Why, my lord, it's a pleasure to see you again."

"And you, my lady. Your return to London makes the City bearable."

Lady Wilthrop fluttered her fan. "While I enjoy the rustic life of the West Country, I always look forward to my return to London."

Ellanor looked at Lady Wilthrop in surprise. There was nothing at all rustic about her neighbor's country home.

"Lord Saxby, may I present my guest, Miss Ellanor Fitzhugh."

Ellanor curtsied.

"Enchanted." Lord Saxby bowed over Ellanor's hand. "With your permission, I present my son, Sir Henry." He put his hand under the elbow of a boy about Ellanor's age and propelled him forward.

Sir Henry Willingham, the future Lord Saxby, pulled his coat straight before bowing to Lady Wilthrop and then to Ellanor. He glanced at his father, who gave him an approving nod.

Lord Saxby nudged his son.

Sir Henry cleared his throat. "Perhaps you'll allow me the pleasure of bringing you a cool drink?" He asked the question as though he had memorized it especially for the occasion.

"I . . . ummm . . . yes, if you please," Ellanor said.

Sir Henry turned on his heel and left on his errand.

"Didn't want to come, you know. Prefers riding and hunting to parties." Lord Saxby watched his son's progress across the hall. "Still, he's quite a lad, my boy." He turned back to Lady Wilthrop. "I'd best see to him. He just might run out the door on me." He chuckled and started after his son.

Lady Wilthrop arranged a bit of lace at her wrist. "You've just met your first potential suitor who will be the fifth Earl of Saxby. Of the northern nobility. I don't think Sir Henry's coming back." She and Ellanor both struggled not to laugh out loud.

Not long after, a baronet bowed over Ellanor's hand and asked her to walk with him through the gallery.

"Of course," said Lady Wilthrop. "A turn through the gallery will refresh us before we attend the masque."

The gallery held portraits and busts of people dressed in the richest of clothes, but whom Ellanor was sure had never relaxed in their lives. Not a smile on any lip, no twinkle in any eye.

The masque was no more exciting. It told of a poor but lovely shepherdess who found true love in the person of a handsome, but rather empty-headed shepherd.

"Did you enjoy the masque?" the baronet asked as they left the room.

Ellanor thought for a moment. "The costumes were exquisite."

"Is that all? I found it quite touching how they eventually found love."

"The story isn't true, you know." Ellanor thought of the men who cared for her father's flocks. "Shepherds never dress in fine silks with ribbons, and they seldom have time to sit around and sing."

Her escort lifted an eyebrow. "Really? I'd have thought it was an easy day in the fields. No work at all, really. Children do it, don't they? Mind you," he went on, "I've never been to the country. Couldn't tolerate the boredom. London's the place for me unless, of course, one wishes to travel in Europe."

Ellanor half-listened to his account of Rome in the autumn. She held her fan to hide a yawn and nearly walked into a man standing directly in front of her.

"John Verleigh, Earl of Netherfield, at your service." He smiled and bowed over Ellanor's hand before turning to her escort. "Sorry to interrupt, Richard, but I have wished to make Miss Fitzhugh's acquaintance all evening."

Ellanor curtsied. "Good evening, my lord."

"I also have instructions from my Aunt Esancy to rescue her from all who tell dull tales of traveling in Europe." Lord Netherfield grinned at the baronet. "Sorry to intrude, my friend, but I have my orders."

The baronet bowed. "Hello, John. I should have known you'd soon turn up. Ah, well, I take my leave for the moment, Mistress Fitzhugh, and hope to renew our conversation at some later time."

She curtsied before turning to her new escort. "My lord? You know Sir Richard well?"

"Very well. We grew up together. He's a fine fellow, but he tends to go on."

Ellanor laughed. "He does, a bit. Thank you and Lady Esancy. You are her grand nephew?"

"The same at your service," he said. "Obviously, my aunt has been introducing me again."

"Well, yes, at Lady Wilthrop's not too long ago, it was. Though I didn't know who you were until this moment."

Lord Netherfield looked both surprised and pleased. "An honest and straightforward woman! Truly a rare find. . . . It's nearly midnight, time for supper. Will you allow me to escort you?"

Ellanor hesitated. "Perhaps I should tell Lady Wilthrop."

"She knows that I came to rescue you from Richard. She's met some friends and will join us later."

"My lord . . . Netherfield? I would be honored to accompany you to supper." Ellanor placed her hand on his arm.

"I imagine some of my own friends are annoyed with me right now," he said as he guided her through the crowds.

"Really, my lord?"

"Quite. They were arguing over who would escort you to supper. While they argued, I approached Lady Wilthrop and requested the privilege. I believe there's a fable about a like incident."

"Aesop wrote one such."

Lord Netherfield's eyebrows rose. "You've read Aesop? Splendid." He led Ellanor back through the gallery. The portraits and busts continued to stare with expressions of grim disapproval. Lord Netherfield's gaze followed Ellanor's.

"They look glum, but they weren't always so dour." he said. "Lady Hilten for example. Why, the stories I've heard about her parties. Royalty fairly begged to be included." Lord Netherfield pointed to another portrait. "That's old Uncle Humphrye. See his sly look? He'd think this evening wants a bit of livening up. Once, when he was visiting in the country, he went for an early ride. When he returned, everyone else was still abed, so he rode his horse into the house. He woke everyone with the clatter and his shouts."

Ellanor laughed. "Really, my lord?"

"That's what my father told me."

"How do you kn—Oh! You said 'Uncle Humphrye.' These are your family?"

His Lordship nodded. "The Earl of Somerset is one of my uncles."

They entered the hall where tables had been set for supper. The guests applauded and cheered when servants paraded in carrying the first course.

The Earl leaned toward Ellanor so she could hear him. "The city of Wells, isn't that near Lady Wilthrop's country home?"

Ellanor nodded. "Yes. My family's lands are neighbor to hers. The Baron and my father were close friends."

"Aunt Esancy looks forward to Lady Wilthrop's return to London every winter. . . . You are visiting Lady Wilthrop?"

"Her ladyship has graciously invited me to London to . . ." Ellanor hesitated, ". . . to chaperone my first winter in society."

His lordship ignored her hesitation. "Then you'll be here all winter? I'm certain you'll have a successful season with many engagements."

"Thank you, my lord."

They ate in silence for a few minutes. Ellanor wondered if she should say something. Lord Netherfield spoke first.

"May I have the pleasure of calling on you some afternoon? We could ride into the countryside. That is, if you ride?"

"Oh, yes! It's been days since I've been out. Charlemagne probably doesn't remember me."

"Charlemagne? Your horse? I shall most definitely call on you, and we'll make a day of it. Have dinner at an inn I know of. Provided the weather holds."

"That would be wonderful. Oh, yes . . ." Ellanor caught herself and began again. "Please do call, my lord. I look forward to your company and a gallop in the country."

Lord Netherfield laughed. "I quite like the first you to the formal you. I'm sure it was all those manners that made those lords and ladies in the gallery so glum."

"I'm supposed to practice at every opportunity." Ellanor sighed. "It's difficult to remember everything."

"I compliment you on your effort. But, please, I'd like to talk with someone who has read Aesop and, I hope, some other worthy authors."

It was nearly two in the morning when Lady Wilthrop called for her coach. She pulled a heavy blanket over her lap. "Did you enjoy yourself?" she asked Ellanor.

"Oh, yes! It was wonderful. That is after Lord Netherfield rescued me from Sir Richard."

"I thought you might appreciate that."

"He was pleasant enough, but a trifle dull."

"Sir Richard's father bought his baronetcy from James I not so long ago. You will do much better than that."

Ellanor chuckled. "I wonder where poor Sir Henry, the future Earl of Saxby, disappeared to."

"Probably fled just as his father thought he would." Lady Wilthrop shook her head. "Poor boy. You enjoyed Lord Netherfield's company?"

Ellanor nodded. "Oh, yes. We talked about his family. Did you know he's the grand nephew of Lady Esancy? He's also the nephew of the Earl of Somerset. Then we talked about books. But, if Lady Esancy is so wealthy, why is he poor?"

"Be assured, his lordship did not destroy his father's fortune. He's doing all he can to recover what was lost."

"I hope he succeeds."

"Do you wish to see him again?"

Ellanor nodded. "He asked if he might call to take me riding."

"In this weather?" Lady Wilthrop shivered. "We'll have to find you a hardier chaperone."

CHAPTER ELEVEN

LORD NETHERFIELD'S LIBRARY

The night of the Earl of Somerset's masque and supper, Lord Wetherby called on an old friend. He knew Lord Netherfield was at Lord Somerset's, but he was willing to wait.

The house was large and even grand in appearance from the outside. The interior, however, gave evidence of the family's declining fortunes. Threadbare carpeting covered the floor. Well-worn furniture filled the rooms. The whole house reminded Lord Wetherby of a country manor last refurbished during the reign of Queen Elizabeth.

An aged and long-time member of the household opened the door.

"Good evening, James," said Wetherby.

"Good evening, my lord." James stood aside for the guest.

"John not home yet?" Lord Wetherby stepped inside.

"I'm sorry to say that he is not. Would you like to wait for his lordship?"

"I would." Lord Wetherby took off his hat and gloves and placed them on a small table. He draped his cloak over a chair. He was sure James was just as happy not to have to deal with them. The old man appeared to be staying up only to unlock the front door for his master. James led him into the library.

"Will you require anything, sir?"

"I think not. I'll let John in."

"I couldn't allow you to do that, sir. I'll be at the back of the house. Should you wish anything, ring the bell."

"I will, thank you."

Lord Wetherby prodded the dying fire. Sparks flew up the chimney. He added some lumps of coal and watched as the flames spread slowly to them.

The library also bore witness to the financial difficulties of Lord Netherfield. The brocade curtains were mended at the edges and hems. The furniture showed dents and scratches from long use.

Only the books were better kept. Closed cabinets kept his friend's library in order. Lord Wetherby opened one of the doors. The number of volumes was growing. Some were in Latin, French, and Italian. John really should spend less on books and buy a new chair or two, thought Lord Wetherby.

A coach clattered past the house, but did not slow. John must have enjoyed himself tonight, he thought. He usually leaves parties early.

He wandered to his friend's writing table. There was a book of household accounts and some lease indentures. The dates on the leases showed they would soon be renegotiated. Good, thought Lord Wetherby. It's about time John is able to revalue some of his leases. That will help him out financially.

Beside a letter book and under a candlestick lay several papers. His lordship was about to turn away when a signature caught his eye. He lit the candle then slid the papers aside one by one. He pursed his lips in a silent whistle, for most of the papers bore the signature of John Pym, the radical leader of the recently elected Parliament.

Lord Wetherby picked up the papers and carried them to a chair by the fire. He read arguments against the King's right to levy taxes and for the authority of Parliament to limit the powers of the crown. Mr. Pym's faction was also considering the impeachment of the King's closest advisers.

Oh, John, my friend, he thought, you've dipped your hand into muddy waters without knowing all that lies below the surface. Have a care. Best you pull back before you fall into matters far too deep for a beginner. Lord Wetherby shook his head. Even if you mean no harm, the Court might question your loyalty. It's a short step to the loss of royal favor. You'd best be careful whom you call *friend.*

Lord Wetherby froze.

James's shuffling footsteps hesitated outside the library door. But when he entered the room, he found his master's best friend sitting by the fire, feet propped on a stool, head back, snoring.

"My lord? I am sorry to disturb you."

Lord Wetherby stirred and yawned. "Fell asleep there for a moment."

"I'm afraid Master John is later than I thought he might be. Is there anything you wish? I could make up a room for you."

"Nothing, thank you, nothing at all. You may retire, James. Certainly, Lord Netherfield will have no need to call on you this evening."

James bowed. "Very good, my lord. You have only to ring should you require anything."

Lord Wetherby waited until the house was silent before he pulled the papers from behind his back. He straightened their edges and put them back on the table. He blew out the candle and replaced it. He hoped James hadn't noticed it had been lighted.

At the sound of horses' hooves on the cobbled street, Lord Wetherby stepped back and surveyed his work. Looks as it did. John will never know. Still . . . he looked a second time, just to make sure. Then he went to the door to greet the master of the house.

"Good evening, or should I say, good morning."

"Edmund? Good to see you. I say, look at my shoes! Ruined they are. And after only one wearing."

John ushered his guest back into the house.

"I sent James to bed. He's really much too old to deal with your comings and goings."

"I'll bet he ignored you. Has quite a mind of his own, does James. Believes it's his duty to see me safely in."

"Your driver put you down in the muddiest part of the street?"

John snorted in disgust. He tugged one shoe off then the other and let both fall. Mud spattered the carpet.

"There was a day when I'd have had four boys at the door all begging to remove my shoes for me. Where is young Alan? You've sent him to bed as well, have you? Go through to the library, Edmund. I'll join you presently." John padded down the hall in his stocking feet.

Lord Wetherby went back into the library without glancing at the desk. He twitched the heavy brocade curtains to assure they were closed, then poked the fire and added more lumps of coal. There certainly is something to be said for servants, he thought as he rubbed his hands together to remove the coal dust. Ah, well, even Alan couldn't coax a better fire than this.

"Nothing like a good fire and a cozy room." John elbowed his way through the door balancing a tray with coffeepot, hot milk, sugar bowl, cups and saucers. "And to make the night complete, a cup of coffee. Just made, and it smells wonderful. Shove those papers aside, will you?" He set the tray on the desk.

They sat in front of the fire with their feet stretched toward it, their coffee cups on a small table between them.

"Found your slippers, I see." Edmund nodded.

"Yes, James left them for me by the kitchen fire. They're old and comfortable."

"The best kind."

John sipped his coffee and stared into the fire. After a few moments he turned to his friend. "I wish you'd not mention those papers to anyone."

Edmund's cup paused in midair. "I beg your pardon?"

"The papers I asked you to move."

"Never noticed. Creditors?"

"Always. But those papers . . ." John nodded toward his writing table, "well, you'd not have found them in my hands a year ago."

Edmund's cup continued its journey. He sipped his coffee. "I'm intrigued. Do go on."

"There are bits and pieces of information one hears—I'm looking further into Parliament's arguments against the King."

"I leave you to your privacy. I've no wish to pry."

"There's really no secret. You know John Pym, friend of my family. My father knew his father and so on."

"Isn't he the leader of the radicals in Parliament?"

"He is. In fact, I posted a letter to him not long ago. I thought his faction was moving too quickly, going too far. He sent some pamphlets along with his comments by return post.

"Many are distressed with the Court, but few dare publish their arguments."

John loosened his cravat. "There is a growing number willing to argue their points publicly. Just look at my desk."

Edmund spoke slowly. "And have you changed your mind regarding the King's authority?"

"I have read all Pym sent me. Some pamphlets I threw in the fire where they deserved to go. Others I'm still considering."

"May I ask which ones?"

"Well, for one, Parliament's demanding that it be called at least once every three years. No more of the King ruling by himself for eleven years. Then there's a bill for doing away with the prerogative courts. Well, I can't argue there. One can't even speak in one's defense in those courts. Not English, that. And thank goodness they've gone after the taxes the King has illegally collected these past years."

"If they are the King's taxes levied by the King, can they be illegal?"

"In the case of ship money, the whole country knows it's illegal."

"Might these new ideas of Parliament not lead to charges of, dare I say, treason?"

John set his cup down with a clatter. "Treason! I tell you, Edmund, the King himself has nearly ruined the country. Those taxes of his may have already destroyed me financially. Someone has to stop it. And it isn't just the taxes. This business of taking a knighthood if you have forty shillings to your name. Perhaps it was necessary during the wars with France two hundred years ago. But now? Knights don't fight wars any more."

"I agree that knighthood is all honorary these days. Safer, too, for the country, at least in your case. You barely know which is the sharp end of the sword."

Lord Netherfield smiled. "I tried to get the knack of sword play when I was at University. All bouncing and dancing about trying to slice one's opponent into decorative bits. Good exercise, but otherwise a waste of time."

"Best you quit when you did."

"But the cost of the knighthood! I'm sure my money went to some royal folly. And if I hadn't taken the knighthood, the court would have demanded a huge fine."

"Is it wise to speak so openly against the King? The walls have ears, you know. Heads have decorated London Bridge for saying less."

"I haven't said anything new. It's all the topic in the coffee houses."

"Still, one could lose His Majesty's favor." Edmund studied the bottom of his coffee cup. "A dangerous thing to lose. . . . How much were you out of pocket for your knighthood? That is, if I'm not intruding too far."

John sat forward in his chair so he could poke at the fire. "At least two thousand pounds. And I had to borrow much of that."

"Really! I hadn't realized the fees for the ceremony were so high."

"Fortunately, most of my creditors are willing to wait. Some of my tenant's leases are up for renewal. If any of my business ventures fail . . . well, I hate to think of the future."

"If there were any way I could help?"

John shook his head. "No. No more loans. However," he stretched and settled back, "I must find a ready source of money."

"And your father? Does he know of all this?" Edmund asked.

"He knows nothing. He hasn't many years left, and his mind is now as feeble as his body. He has no idea what his schemes have cost the family."

"And you, as the good son, will keep it from him. Ventures in the New World are always a risk."

"Indeed. And he lived beyond his means for many years. But then, what family doesn't?" John smiled. "Speaking of ready money, I made it a point to meet Lady Wilthrop's latest social offering. I thought I might as well since my Aunt Esancy prepared the way for me."

"Doesn't Lady Wilthrop bring eligible young women to London for their first season?"

"Eligible and wealthy. She, herself, brought money to her marriage and reversed her husband's fortunes. Married her own daughters, or perhaps it was her nieces, very well. Now it appears she helps other families do the same."

"Whom is she chaperoning this winter?" Edmund slid further down in his chair.

"A Miss Ellanor Fitzhugh. Her family is from the west, near Wells. Owns a tidy bit of land."

"Fitzhugh. I don't recall the name."

"Humble beginnings and all that. Did exceptionally well in trade. He could probably buy a baronetcy outright."

"Or have his daughter marry a coronet. Quite a step up for a merchant. Are you going to call on Mistress Fitzhugh?"

John rubbed his hands together. "Seriously? I've asked, but how far it can go I don't know. She's fair enough. Red curly hair and gray eyes. Not exceptionally pretty until she smiles. Well read in the classics. She's young, though, a child really."

"What's age? The King's daughter is but nine and, in May, she'll wed William of Orange who's barely twelve."

"That's all politics and alliances, isn't it? I'd like my marriage to be more, to rest on some mutual regard."

"You ask a lot."

"Perhaps."

"Lady Wilthrop's girl will, no doubt, come with a handsome dowry."

"Yes, and I'm tempted. But I don't think I could marry a child, or anyone else, for that matter, for money."

Edmund saluted his friend and stood. "I wish you good fortune in your endeavors. It's late, and I must be on my way."

"Glad you called 'round, Edmund. It's been too long since we've had an evening, or should I say, an early morning."

The two men walked to the door. Lord Wetherby shook his friend's hand before stepping into his waiting coach.

DERBYSHIRE

"Mistress, you are to join Lady Wilthrop for dinner." Priscilla closed the door behind her.

"Come and watch the storm." Ellanor stood by the window. Clouds swept across the sky. Trees bent before the wind. When the rain finally came, it sounded like gravel hitting the window.

"Aren't you glad you don't have to go out this evening?"

"Ummm. Look at that man. He can barely keep his cloak around him. There goes his hat." Ellanor shivered and pulled the heavy draperies together.

"There won't be any guests for dinner tonight." Priscilla peeked through the curtains.

"I wonder why Lady Wilthrop wants me to join her."

Priscilla shrugged. "What would you like to wear?"

"Something warm."

Half an hour later, Priscilla draped a shawl over Ellanor's shoulders and stood back to admire the effect. "Lovely. That shade of green suits you. I'll be in my room when you return."

After dinner, Lady Wilthrop led Ellanor from the dining room. "We'll have our dessert in the drawing room," she said.

Lady Wilthrop and Ellanor entered just as Fines finished stirring the fire. He bowed himself from the room and returned almost immediately with a tray full of cups, saucers, a teapot, a spice cake, and a pitcher of hot custard.

"Well, my dear," said Lady Wilthrop, "we have this evening to ourselves. And such weather! I believe I would have sent regrets had we any engagements."

"Priscilla and I watched some poor man chase after his hat."

"Are you and Priscilla warm in your rooms?"

"As long as we keep the draperies closed and the fire stirred up."

"What do you think of your first winter in London?" Lady Wilthrop asked.

Ellanor sat down and smoothed her skirts. "It's certainly colder here than at home. It's been wonderful. I've never had so many beautiful clothes. And most of the people have been kind." She looked at her patroness and wrinkled her forehead. "What do we do now?"

Lady Wilthrop poured the tea and served the cake. "I beg your pardon?"

"Well, I've been to what seems like dozens of afternoon gatherings and the Earl of Somerset's party."

"Yes?"

"And nothing has happened. I mean, no one seems interested." Ellanor poured custard over her cake.

"You thought your search for a husband would be over quickly?"

"Father says it isn't that difficult to find a poor nobleman these days."

Lady Wilthrop laughed out loud. "Oh my dear, forgive me. I'm not laughing at you, really, but you sounded so like your father just then." She dabbed at the corner of an eye with her handkerchief. "We've only begun. Introducing you this winter is our most important work. That and your lessons." Lady Wilthrop paused. "Both you and Priscilla have come along exceptionally well."

Ellanor smiled. She'd heard "Ladies don't do . . ." much less frequently of late.

Lady Wilthrop set her plate on the tray. "I have some news for you. All of your afternoons have had pleasant results."

Ellanor sipped her tea. "Pleasant results?"

Lady Wilthrop held up several pieces of heavy paper. "When you next write to your parents, you must tell them of the many invitations to holiday celebrations you've received. Each of these asks for the pleasure of your company. I thought you might enjoy choosing which to accept." Lady Wilthrop handed the invitations to Ellanor. "Please, read them, and see if any appeal."

Ellanor read through each invitation. "I shall send my regrets to Lord Saxby, that is, if you approve. I think his son greets me only because his father says he must. . . . May I accept Lady Esancy's? I always look forward to seeing her, and she is always kind to me."

"I was rather hoping you would choose that one. You do realize this is a house party? We shall be at her estate for several days."

"Her estate?"

"In Derbyshire. It's been in her husband's family for generations."

"Who will be there?"

"I have no idea, but many who desire an invitation never receive one. You, my dear, are fortunate. She must regard you most affectionately. I'll send our acceptance immediately."

The last days of November passed quickly into December. The winds off the North Sea drove snow over London, leaving its streets clean and white until passing coach and cart wheels turned the snow dirty gray. Only the oldest citizens could recall another winter as cold. Lady Wilthrop added heavier clothes to the trunks she sent ahead to Derbyshire.

On the coldest morning of early winter, Fines handed Lady Wilthrop, Ellanor, Martha, and Priscilla into Lady Wilthrop's coach. The women wore thick, fur-lined cloaks and boots. Hot bricks wrapped in heavy cloth nearly covered the coach floor. As soon as the coach turned into the Strand, Fines hurried indoors.

The crunch of wheels on frozen gravel filled the brittle air. The beat of horses hooves punctuated the creak of leather harness. Ellanor huddled in the cushions of the swaying coach, her cloak tucked around her against the cold. How good it felt to be out of the City, to see open fields, to breathe fresh air so cold it froze the inside of her nose when she took a deep breath.

She rubbed the frost from the coach window. Frozen stalks and withered leaves lined the road and reflected the white-gold of the cold morning sun. A stone wall glistered silver-gray with frost. Patches of old snow glowed dimly under hedgerows.

Dusk had fallen on the fourth day when the outriders' "halloo" announced their arrival at Lady Esancy's estate. Inside the mansion's ancient oak doors, warmth flowed around them. Servants took their gloves, scarves, and cloaks.

Lady Esancy stepped forward. "Welcome, welcome. You've come in spite of the cold. I was hoping it wouldn't put you off."

Lady Wilthrop curtsied to her hostess. "Thank you for your kind invitation, my lady. It was most gracious of you to remember us."

Lady Esancy turned to Ellanor. "And you, my dear. I'm delighted to welcome you."

Ellanor curtsied. "Thank you, my lady. I'm happy to see you again as well."

"No doubt you wish to refresh yourselves. Your maids are on their way to your chambers." Lady Esancy nodded to two maids who stepped forward. "These girls will wait on your pleasure while you are here. If you have need of anything, you have only to ask. Give your own maids a bit of a holiday. Please join me in the Italian parlor when you have rested."

One of the maids curtsied to Ellanor. "Miss? Follow me, if you please." She guided Ellanor through the twists and turns of the old mansion and stopped before a finely carved door. "This is your chamber, Miss. If you'll excuse me, I'll help your maid finish unpacking."

"Thank you. What's your name?" Ellanor asked.

"Emily, miss. Emily Fowler. Should you desire anything, please call me."

"I'll need you as a guide to the Italian parlor, Emily. I'm completely lost."

CHAPTER 12 *Ellanor's Exchange*

Emily laughed. "This old country house has seen many additions. Don't worry; I'll keep you out of the scullery."

In less than an hour Ellanor rejoined Lady Esancy.

"Sit down, my dear. You're the first to arrive." Lady Esancy pulled Ellanor down beside her. "This will warm you up," she said as a servant handed Ellanor a cup of hot cider.

"This is the Italian parlor?" Ellanor looked around.

"It's named for that statue over there." Lady Esancy nodded toward a statue of a Roman lady carved from creamy white marble. "My husband and I saw it when we traveled in Italy years ago. I thought it so lovely that the Earl purchased it and had it brought to England. We put it here, and this room has been the Italian parlor ever since. . . . Please, excuse me."

Lady Esancy rose to greet other guests.

When Lady Wilthrop entered the parlor, Ellanor joined her.

"Let's stand over here and see who has arrived." Lady Wilthrop led Ellanor to one side of the room. "There's William Montfort, Baron of Sorley. His family is from Sussex. He's gruff as an old bear, but he means no harm. Ah, Lady Durston, the one in light blue. If you play at cards with her, you'll find that she cheats horribly. She's such a delightful old thing that no one really minds. Besides, she almost never wins. . . . The gentleman warming himself at the fire is her husband. He loves a good joke. His laugh can be heard from one end of the house to the other. And over there—" Lady Wilthrop continued her commentary until a friend drew her into conversation.

Ellanor did not stand alone for long. Lady Durston bustled across the room and introduced herself. "My dear, would you help make up a table for a game of whist tomorrow evening? You must join us. You will sit across from me and we shall be partners." Lady Durston tapped Ellanor's arm with her fan. "We shall have quite a good time, though I almost never win. Perhaps you'll bring me luck."

The next morning the household awoke to several inches of new snow. Ellanor joined Lord and Lady Montfort for a sleigh ride. The snow muffled the thump of horses' hooves and whispered against the runners of the sleigh. Ellanor felt as if she were floating through a silent world of white.

The guests filled each afternoon and evening with games and music. Ellanor played whist with Lady Durston and found that her partner really did cheat. Lord Durston challenged Ellanor to a game of draughts and declared a mismatch when, with a flourish, she removed his last three pieces from the board. Musicians visited from the village, and the guests joined in folk dances. One evening they played Blind Man's Buff, on another, they put on a play.

It was Priscilla who discovered the library and led Ellanor there one morning before the other guests had risen.

"Have you ever seen so many books, Mistress? There must be thousands."

Books lined the room from floor to ceiling. A ladder stood in the corner so books on the upper shelves could be retrieved. Ellanor tilted her head so she could read the titles. "I've found some books of history. They're right next to the ones on how to train dogs and raise cows and sheep. . . . Here's Chaucer, Geoffrey of Monmouth, Bede, even Einhard."

She took down a history of Richard I, Lionheart. Priscilla chose *The Travels of Marco Polo*. The girls pulled two chairs close to the fire and stuffed pillows all around them for comfort and warmth. From time to time a servant entered the room to tend the fire. At eleven o'clock, Emily carried in a tray of hot tea and scones.

Ellanor returned to the library several mornings following. On her fourth visit, she pulled her chair close to the fire and turned it so she could see the snow falling outside. She pulled her heavy shawl close and was soon lost in the tale of Richard I's battles against Philip II of France.

"The fire's been lit, my lord, but the library is still cold."

"I shouldn't wonder. I can't recall a winter like this. Put the tray on the table by the fireplace. That will be all. I shall serve myself."

Ellanor marked her page with her finger and stood to greet the new arrival.

"Excuse me, my lord." Ellanor curtsied. "I am just leaving."

"Eh? What?" Lord Netherfield turned. "Mistress Fitzhugh?"

Ellanor curtsied again. "Yes, my lord. . . . Lord Netherfield?"

"A pleasure to see you. There's no need for you to leave." He held up his hand and went to the library door. "A moment, if you please."

Ellanor heard him speak to someone in the hallway. "I should leave," she said. "Please forgive me for intruding."

"It is I who am intruding. Have you had breakfast? No? Will you join me? There's enough here for four people."

Ellanor shook her head. "Thank you, but I must not. May I take the book with me? I'll see that it's returned."

"If it's a matter of a chaperone—"

One of the housekeepers carrying a basket of embroidery work entered the room. She curtsied to Lord Netherfield and went to sit by a window.

"—that is taken care of. Please join me." He pulled back a chair for Ellanor.

"Thank you, my lord." Ellanor hoped Lady Wilthrop would approve and sat down.

A servant appeared, set another place, and served breakfast.

"Well, then," Lord Netherfield began, "have you enjoyed my Aunt Esancy's Christmas celebrations?"

"Oh, yes, they've been wonderful. I've never seen so much snow; we seldom have any in Somerset. And I've never ridden in a sleigh before. It was so quiet and beautiful."

Lord Netherfield nodded toward one of the library windows. "I've never seen the snow this deep."

Ellanor continued. "It made it easier to pull the yule log to the house. The whole village was here."

"And they didn't leave until the last meat pie and mug of ale disappeared," said his lordship.

"I think it probably took their feet and hands that long to thaw."

"I'm happy all went well."

"There were gifts for everyone and toys for the children."

"They arrived? I hoped they would, but with this weather . . ."

"You've just arrived, my lord?"

"Late last night. I would have come earlier, but the snow delayed me. At one point the road was closed by drifts. My men and I had to clear our own way. Cold work. The wind blew the snow back almost as quickly as we removed it. Did any of the guests have difficulty on the roads?"

"Most of us arrived before the storms."

"Tell me who has come."

Ellanor began listing Lady Esancy's guests. Lord Netherfield interrupted her. "Lady Durston's here? I haven't seen her for over a year. She's another of my aunts on my father's side."

Ellanor laughed. "You know, she cannot play whist at all."

"No, she really cannot." Lord Netherfield shook his head and chuckled.

They finished breakfast just as a servant carried another pot of hot tea to the table.

His lordship sent a cup of tea and a scone to the housekeeper who smiled a thank you from her chair. He and Ellanor moved closer to the fire and drank their tea while the table was cleared.

"I never knew the nobility could be so friendly," Ellanor said. "They are all quite proper in London and sometimes rather boring."

"I'm happy we've changed your mind. Now you see it won't be so terrible marrying into a title."

Ellanor felt her face turning red. She stared at the tea cup she held in her lap.

"Don't be embarrassed, Mistress Fitzhugh. Young women of wealthy family frequently come to London to marry into a noble house. And it's a good thing they do because many a noble family would otherwise sink to terrible poverty. You must have known when we met at Lord Somerset's that I, myself, am out-of-pocket. Surely my aunt mentioned my current condition."

"Not Lady Esancy; it was Lady Wilthrop," said Ellanor. "But I truly forgot. You never acted as if you were . . ."

"Poor?"

Ellanor looked up and nodded.

"It's true." Lord Netherfield propped his feet on a stool. "I must find a way to recover my family's fortunes. Marriage to a wealthy woman is probably the easiest way."

"How," asked Ellanor, "can noble families be poor? After all, they own so much land. Father says it's most likely the result of poor estate management."

Lord Netherfield didn't move for several seconds. "I've never heard it put quite so plainly," he said.

Ellanor stared hard at her tea cup. "Please, forgive me my lord. I didn't mean to imply that you—"

Lord Netherfield cleared his throat and continued, "Our misfortune was a bit different. Perhaps some would say it was mismanagement; our ventures to the New World failed. Evidently the shores are not scattered with gold and gems as some have said."

Ellanor answered in a whisper. "Father says many fail. A year ago he lost two shiploads of salted and dried fish, one to a storm, the other to pirates."

Lord Netherfield looked over at Ellanor. "Dried fish?" His frown dissolved into laughter. "Can you imagine pirates getting a shipload of fish?"

"It must have been a great disappointment." Ellanor smiled and felt her shoulders relax a little. "Father says they probably got a good price for it in the Antilles, though." She looked over at her host. "Please, forgive me, my lord. I too often speak out of turn . . ."

His lordship refilled their cups. Their spoons clinked lightly against the cups as they stirred sugar into their tea. Ellanor noticed that large snowflakes were once again drifting past the window.

"Mistress Ellanor, perhaps it is I who should apologize. I confess I have often looked down on merchants and the wealth that seems to come so easily to their pockets. I'm ashamed to say that I often held them in contempt."

"Contempt, my lord?"

Lord Netherfield went on. "Merchants scorn us for our debt; we look down on them when they become wealthy and wish a title. It seems we are both guilty of the same attitude."

"Each dislikes the other, but each is willing to use the other to get what he wants," said Ellanor.

"Overall, not a flattering picture." His lordship drank his tea.

Ellanor watched the falling snow. She spoke softly. "A title is Father's greatest desire. My brother Paul was to marry into the nobility. When he died suddenly, Father placed his hopes on me. I never wished it. I do not wish it now."

Lord Netherfield studied Ellanor's profile. "You don't want to marry into the nobility?"

"Not like this. Such a marriage would be little more than a business arrangement. Father's wealth for a coronet. Gold for gold. A fair exchange, one might say."

"But, your children, think of their future. They would inherit your husband's title. It would establish the name of Fitzhugh for generations to come."

Ellanor looked at her host. "That's true. But what of me? Must I marry someone for the future only? Can't I be happy . . . in the same way my parents are? Much more than money and social position binds them together."

Lord Netherfield gave a deep sigh. "You are right. Gold and titles make a narrow foundation on which to build a marriage. Neither one of us is in an enviable position."

Ellanor glanced out the window again. "No."

The library was still except for the hiss and crackle of the logs in the fireplace. A series of pops launched ash and glowing coals onto the hearth.

Lord Netherfield stirred. "Remember, however, it was our unhappy conditions that brought us together at Lord Somerset's. We should be grateful for that. I enjoyed escorting you to supper."

"Yes, I had a wonderful time."

"After the first three courses, I didn't think about your father's money at all."

"Not even from time to time?"

"Not that evening. Though I've thought about it since."

"Now you're laughing at me."

"Not at all. And can you say you never thought of my title?"

"My lord, I was relieved and happy to be rescued from Sir Richard."

Lord Netherfield nodded in understanding. "His stories can tire the most dedicated listener." His lordship turned to Ellanor. "It was Aunt Esancy who told me to pry you away from him. I wonder if she and your Lady Wilthrop have been busy behind our backs."

"Surely not, my lord."

"You don't know my aunt. She's been trying to marry me off for over four years, bless her."

"I don't think it will work, my lord. We aren't suited."

Lord Netherfield wrinkled his brow. "I beg your pardon?"

"Well, to begin with, neither of us wants to be forced into marriage, and there is a great difference in our ages."

"How old are you?"

"Fifteen last month."

"I'm but twenty-three."

"As I said, a great difference. And I don't have the regard for you I hope to have for my husband."

"So you would refuse me, Mistress Fitzhugh?"

Ellanor nodded. "Right now, I would refuse anybody."

"You won't refuse me as a friend, I hope."

"Oh, no. We should remain friends."

Lord Netherfield sat forward in his chair. "Then let's ignore, for the time at least, the wishes and wants of our families. Let's agree to enjoy each other's company without any claims against the future. What do you say?"

"Is that possible? Won't people comment?"

"Let them. This is our agreement."

"How long is it to last?"

Lord Netherfield shrugged. "Who knows? But it will give me some time to reconsider my attitude towards merchants and their daughters."

"And I can learn more about the nobility as they really are. . . . All right, my lord. I accept. It will be good to have a friend who isn't always wondering who I'll marry."

Lord Netherfield nodded, stood, and offered his arm. "Come, friend Mistress Fitzhugh. I hear others stirring."

LUCY HAY,
COUNTESS OF CARLISLE

"Mary, it's been far too long." Lady Carlisle held out her hands to Lady Wilthrop.

"And, you, Lucy. I seldom see you. Are you so busy at Court?"

Lady Carlisle led them to seats close to the fire. "Indeed. You've heard of the proposed marriage treaty between Princess Mary and William of Orange? Her Majesty sent me as her personal representative when the delegation delivered the marriage contract to the Netherlands. It's so good to be home." The ladies laughed and talked about their families, the weather, and the holiday season just past.

Ellanor hardly dared move. She sat with her hands folded in her lap. Here I am, she thought, in the home of the Queen's closest friend. I wonder what it's like to talk to Her Majesty almost every day? What do they talk about?

"Ellanor?"

"Yes, Lady Carlisle?"

"You are exactly as Lady Wilthrop described you. I hope you have enjoyed your stay in London."

"I have indeed, Lady Carlisle."

Lady Carlisle turned to Lady Wilthrop. "How ever did you hear that I wanted a companion? I told no one outside the Court."

"Lord Limbourne visited one morning, completely unannounced. He was extremely eager that I should hear the news and take immediate advantage."

"How curious!"

"Not really. I believe I understand his motive."

"I must hear this, but how boring for Ellanor. . . . Ellanor, would you care to see my home?"

"May I? Oh, yes, please."

A servant stepped forward. "This is Jenny. She will guide you. When you return, please join us in the small withdrawing room."

Ellanor curtsied and followed her guide out of the room.

Lady Carlisle dismissed the other servants with a nod. When all the doors were closed, she motioned Lady Wilthrop to join her on a couch in the center of the room.

"What's this, then?" Lady Wilthrop left her chair by the fire.

Her friend put her finger to her lips and patted the seat beside her.

Lady Wilthrop sat beside her friend.

"I like to be as far away from doors and windows as possible." Lady Carlisle spoke softly.

"Whatever fo—?" Lady Wilthrop looked at the doors and then at the windows. "Surely not! I've heard of such goings on at Court but—"

"I am certain that at least one of my servants is less than completely loyal."

"Why? What possible reason could there be?"

Lady Carlisle waved her hand in the air as if batting away a bothersome insect. "My dear, there's always the odd bit of scandal to be overheard and spread abroad."

"I'm sure you'll soon sort them out." Lady Wilthrop moved closer to her friend.

Lady Carlisle sat quietly for a moment. When she spoke, it was as if she had reached a difficult decision.

"My dear Mary," she said, "there's more to this than an unfaithful servant or two. I must talk to someone. It weighs on my mind constantly."

"Oh, my."

"Speak softly." Lady Carlisle reminded her. "My position at Court is not as comfortable as I would wish. There have been insinuations against me. Forgive me, I should begin at the beginning." Lady Carlisle took a deep breath. "The Queen considers me her closest friend and gives me her complete confidence. It's quite an honor, but she does rattle on. I assure you, most of what she says is of no consequence."

"Perhaps she's lonely? After all, you speak French so very well."

"This goes far beyond Her Majesty's delight in speaking her own language. When I say she rattles on, I mean she tells me absolutely everything. I know every detail about everything from the children to, well, affairs of state. Just last week she told me of the letters she'd written to the Catholics in England asking for contributions to support the King while he's visiting Scotland. He's forever in need of money, you know."

"To Catholics? For money? Surely Parliament did not like that."

"When they discovered what she'd done, they forced Her Majesty to apologize. I still can't quite believe it." Lady Carlisle looked at her guest as if daring her to imagine such an offense. "And, that's not all. Two or three days later she whispers to me that she's also written to Richelieu and the Pope for money to protect Roman Catholics here in England!"

Lady Wilthrop stared at her hostess. "That's treason! She's playing a dangerous game!"

"Shhh! To make matters worse, for the last few months, the King's most closely kept decisions are no longer secret. They are known to his enemies almost immediately. I'm certain that I am under suspicion."

"Who could possibly suggest that you don't keep the Queen's confidence?"

"The Commander of the King's Guard."

"Of course, you've never—"

"No, never. I wouldn't think of it."

"What makes you think you aren't trusted?"

"Only a week ago I overheard Lord Wetherby demand of the Queen that she remove me from her service. Her Majesty became so angry with him, that he withdrew."

Lady Wilthrop turned to Lady Carlisle. "Who did you say?"

"Lord Wetherby. You know him?"

"I know of him, little more. Please, go on."

"The King appointed him Commander of the Guard about a year ago. He took no formal military rank. Indeed, I believe his appointment is a well-guarded secret. Many would refuse to speak to him if they knew of his position and the power it gives him."

"Perhaps he should seek treason in the King's household rather than in the Queen's."

"I wish he would. He has found nothing. And he won't!" Lady Carlisle's hands clenched tightly over a lace handkerchief. "Of course, he'll keep on searching. It's his duty to His Majesty."

Lady Wilthrop leaned closer to her friend. "You believe a member of your household reports to him?"

"When I see two of my servants whispering in a corner, I want to run and hide. I don't know whom to trust any more." Lady Carlisle pressed her handkerchief to one eye, then the other. "My situation is made even more uncomfortable because Mr. Pym is one of my closest friends."

"The leader of Commons? I say, Lucy, you are in the middle."

"I'm sure Lord Wetherby believes that I pass what the Queen tells me along to Mr. Pym." Tears rolled down Lady Carlisle's cheeks.

"What you say leaves me . . . astonished. Could you leave your service to the Queen?"

"Oh, no. One does not remove oneself from Her Majesty's service. Besides, I've decided that it might appear as though I had something to hide after all. I will not give that man the satisfaction of chasing me away from Her Majesty."

"And so you should not. I think that Lord Wetherby is less than an honorable man."

"I believe my letters have been opened. The seal on the note you sent last November was badly cracked when I received it." Lady Carlisle blinked back more tears.

Lady Wilthrop took her friend's hand, and waited for her to continue.

Finally Lady Carlisle said, "It's a relief to speak with someone I can trust completely. And, I understand if you no longer wish to be associated with me, or if you wish to find another position for Ellanor."

"Not associate with you? That's foolish; you are my dear friend. His lordship is snatching at straws if he believes you guilty of breaking the Queen's confidence."

"Thank you. Your trust is comforting."

"As for Ellanor," Lady Wilthrop hesitated.

"Do you not see why I need a companion such as Ellanor? She has no ties at Court. I tried to find a companion from among the families at Court, but in these difficult times everyone has declared an allegiance."

Lady Wilthrop sat quietly for many moments. When she spoke it was as if she were thinking out loud. "She is so young and open-hearted. I would not like her to be caught up in court intrigue. My responsibility to Ellanor and her family . . ."

"I'll guard her carefully, I assure you. Her Majesty will protect her also."

"Her Majesty?"

"Of course. As my companion, Ellanor would have the Queen's protection."

"Well, that certainly counts for something."

"As for Lord Wetherby, I usually know when he's around. I could keep Ellanor closer at those times. Besides," Lady Carlisle sniffed into her handkerchief, "it doesn't matter what Lord Wetherby thinks or how many spies he may set on me. There's nothing to be found. I'm innocent of any wrong."

"I believe you, Lucy, but I can't make this decision alone. I must write to Master Fitzhugh, explain the situation, and request his permission to place his daughter in your household." Lady Wilthrop nodded. "Yes, that is what must be done. Though I think that whatever her father decides, I will warn Ellanor most sternly to avoid Lord Wetherby. She will listen to me. Ellanor's maid especially doesn't trust him."

The two women sat quietly for a moment. A log rolled off the grate sending a shower of sparks up the chimney. Outside, the wind drove raindrops against the windows.

It was as if Lady Carlisle finally heard her friend's last comment. "Mary, what did you just say?"

"Hmmm? I was just thinking how pleasant this room is in spite of the weather. February is always so—"

"No, about Ellanor's maid . . . and Lord Wetherby?"

"Priscilla doesn't like him at all."

"She knows him? How could she possibly know him?"

Lady Wilthrop smoothed the lace at her wrists. "Well, it's quickly told. Last August when Ellanor and I were traveling to London, we stopped at Bath. You know that lovely inn above the cathedral square? In the afternoon Ellanor and Priscilla were in the garden. They thought themselves alone, but were met by his lordship."

"Really."

"Ellanor said he asked quite a lot of questions about who she was and when she would arrive in London. He left rather abruptly and told her not to mention the meeting to me. Later she asked me whether he had come by to greet me. Evidently he said he would as a surprise. Since I hardly know him, I thought Ellanor had misunderstood, and the incident passed from my mind."

"He was contriving some plan. He always is." Lady Carlisle stood. "Please, don't rise. I simply can't stay seated another minute." She walked around the sitting room. She stopped to remove some wilted petals from a bouquet of flowers and threw the petals into the fire before returning to the couch. "How did he know you were bringing Ellanor to London?"

Lady Wilthrop shrugged. "Well, I have brought other young ladies with me—"

"Yes, but he knew when and where to find you, as well!"

"He was spying on me?"

"Probably one of his lackeys."

"I'm sure I would have noticed someone prowling about."

Lady Carlisle laughed out loud. "Sorry, sorry. No, my dear Mary. You would never have known."

"Oh, my! Circles within circles!" Lady Wilthrop gasped. "You don't suppose . . . Lord Wetherby wouldn't! Would he? He wasn't even then thinking of—"

Lady Carlisle finished the thought, "Using Ellanor to collect information for him? If he could arrange it, yes. I do wonder how he thought she might be useful."

"If nothing else, it explains why a peer of the realm would stop to converse with a common country girl. Lucy, you must promise me you will guard Ellanor ever so closely. I must be able to send the greatest assurances to her father."

"I will keep Ellanor and her maid as far from Wetherby as I can. If it's within my power, they will never meet."

Lady Wilthrop rubbed her forehead with her fingers. "I need a cup of tea. Perhaps two. When will your girl be returning with Ellanor?"

"We needn't wait for them. Jenny will show Ellanor every room in the mansion, and then she'll go to the kitchen for a chat with her mother. . . . Let's go in. . . . I'm curious, Mary. You're sure it wasn't Lord Wetherby who told you of my desire for a companion, was it?"

"Oh, no. It was Lord Limbourne."

Lady Carlisle thought for a moment. "You said so earlier. I'd forgotten. Does he have any association with Lord Wetherby?"

"None that I know of. I believe he was trying to put me in his debt so that I would look more favorably in his direction."

"Do tell!"

"Since the Baron died, Limbourne has been, at times, almost importunate."

"What a nerve! Has he proposed marriage yet?"

"Not yet. I think he fears the answer and prefers to live in hope."

"Let's have that cup of tea."

A few minutes later Jenny returned Ellanor to the small room where a table was laid with hand-painted porcelain dishes and heavy silver table service. Lady Wilthrop and Lady Carlisle were already seated. Jenny seated Ellanor and withdrew.

"You have an elegant home, Lady Carlisle." Ellanor waited for her tea to be poured. "I do believe I've seen it all, except perhaps the storerooms."

"Why, thank you, Ellanor. I thought Jenny would show you every nook. I find it comfortable."

Lady Wilthrop leaned forward. "Lady Carlisle wishes you to join her, for a short time at least, as part of her household. We must, however, have your father's permission."

That evening Ellanor rushed to tell Priscilla all that happened.

"Priscilla, it was so . . ." Ellanor's hands waved through the air.

"Lady Carlisle? What's she like?"

"A great lady. Oh, Priscilla, she's gorgeous. She could be a queen. Her bodice and skirt were of heavy deep blue silk. She had the finest lace at her throat and wrists. Very few jewels. It sounds plain when I describe it, but she was lovely. Her servants know exactly what she wants whenever she so much as lifts her chin in their direction."

Priscilla leaned closer. "What about her apartments?"

"Everything is covered in silks and taffetas. I'm certain the window hangings were silk brocade," Ellanor sighed, "in rose and cream."

Priscilla's "Oh" joined Ellanor's sigh. "I would love to see that."

"And flowers, great bouquets of real flowers, everywhere."

"In February? Where does she get them?"

Ellanor shook her head as if even she could hardly believe what she was telling her maid. "The best part is, I'm going to join her household as her companion."

"Mistress! That's wonderful. . . . How long will you stay?"

Eleanor's Exchange

"I don't know. Lady Wilthrop says she must first write to Father for his permission. I know he'll give it. He has to."

She took her maid's hands in hers and whirled her off the window seat. "And won't it be wonderful when we get there? Yes, you're going, too. You must, you know."

ENTER ROLAND

On the first day of April, Lord Wetherby's plain black coach followed Lady Wilthrop's down the Strand. His informant was right. Ellanor was joining Lady Carlisle's household. Finally, he thought, the girl is in place. All that's left is to turn her into a source of information about Lady Carlisle's activities. Lord Wetherby knocked with his walking stick on the roof of his coach and settled back for the ride to Westminster.

Lady Wilthrop, Ellanor, and Lady Carlisle stood in the entry hall of Lady Carlisle's home. Lady Wilthrop took Ellanor's hands in hers. "My dear, this is far above what I had hoped for you. To be in the household of such a great lady and to accompany her to Court are . . . well, what can I say? Still, I can hardly bear to leave without you; you've become a part of my home."

Ellanor shivered with excitement. "Oh, Lady Wilthrop, all of this . . ." she shook her head as if in disbelief. "I can't imagine . . ."

"Not even my own daughter had such an opportunity. Take every advantage to learn from her ladyship as you serve her."

"Yes, Lady Wilthrop."

"Priscilla, too."

Ellanor nodded.

Lady Wilthrop turned to Lady Carlisle. "I thank you again, Lucy. I know you'll enjoy Ellanor's company."

Lady Carlisle walked arm in arm with her friend. "This will be a delightful distraction for me. I remember when I was young. Now . . . what is Ellanor's age?"

"She turned fifteen last November."

"Fifteen. A wonderful age for any girl. I shall enjoy it again through her." Lady Carlisle gave her friend a quick hug.

They stepped outside. A watery sun tried to banish the damp left by morning showers.

"Visit often," Lady Carlisle continued. "And when you are unable to visit, I shall send to you notes of how Ellanor is getting on. I promise you and Master Fitzhugh, I'll keep her from any who might try to entangle her in court intrigues."

A footman handed Lady Wilthrop into her coach. She waved and disappeared into the busy Strand.

Lady Carlisle personally reviewed Ellanor's and Priscilla's wardrobes. Nothing was suitable for Court. The fashions of last year were not the fashions of this year; besides both girls had grown. Once again they stood for fittings. While the seamstresses cut and stitched, Lady Carlisle taught Ellanor and Priscilla the manners expected at Whitehall Palace. If the girls thought Lady Wilthrop's training was demanding, the refinements Lady Carlisle expected were amazing.

Ellanor and Priscilla also discovered how busy a Lady of the Queen's Chamber was. Almost every day Lady Carlisle attended Her Majesty. A note delivered at any hour of the day or night sent her back to the palace.

"I asked Lady Carlisle if she ever grew tired of waiting on the Queen," Ellanor said to Priscilla one afternoon.

"What did she say?"

"She said that it was an honor and a joy to serve Her Majesty."

Ellanor and Priscilla first entered the Queen's apartments in early June. Lady Carlisle curtsied to a small, beautiful woman with black hair and large, dark eyes. Queen Henrietta Maria immediately drew her confidant aside. Since no one sat unbidden in Her Majesty's presence, Ellanor and Priscilla stood against a wall out of the way of hurrying maids.

"They're all speaking French," Priscilla whispered.

Ellanor nodded, not sure if they should speak.

At first they were fascinated by the Queen and the constant activity around her. After an hour, however, even Ellanor grew bored.

Ellanor felt a tug on her sleeve. Priscilla whispered, "What can they be talking about all this time? Let's stand by the window. We won't be in anyone's way there. If I don't move soon, I shall be frozen in place."

Priscilla was already sliding sideways. Ellanor followed. The Thames flowed past the Queen's chambers. By turning just a little, they could watch the world float by. It reminded Ellanor of their own arrival not quite a year before.

Finally, Lady Carlisle rose and came over to them. "Her Majesty does not require my presence again until tomorrow. We are free to leave." She led them through a maze of rooms and hallways to a large garden. "I must walk a bit. It can be difficult to sit for so long."

After a few minutes Ellanor asked, "Lady Carlisle, may we sit down for a few minutes?"

"Of course, my dear. I quite forgot that you'd been standing all that time." Lady Carlisle nodded to a servant and sent him for a light meal to be served in the garden.

"Priscilla? What are you doing?" Ellanor's maid had collapsed onto a bench and was bent over fumbling with her shoes.

"I just couldn't stand it any longer, Mistress. My ankles started to itch while we were standing inside, and now I must scratch them or die!"

"Straighten up, Priscilla. Quit clawing at your hems." Ellanor looked up at Lady Carlisle to apologize, but her ladyship had taken a seat beside Priscilla and was removing her shoes.

"Oh, the relief. Why are some shoes never comfortable?" She patted the bench beside her. "Come, Ellanor. Relax until the servant returns with our meal."

By the end of June, Ellanor and Priscilla knew their way around the palace well enough to deliver a dinner invitation for Lady Carlisle.

"Mistress Fitzhugh? What an unexpected surprise!"

In spite of Lady Carlisle's best intentions and Lady Wilthrop's warnings, Ellanor could do nothing except stop and greet the Commander of the King's Guard. "My lord." She curtsied.

Lord Wetherby smiled. "I understand you've joined Lady Carlisle's household."

"Indeed, my lord."

"Is her ladyship well?"

"Lady Carlisle is well, thank you."

"I see you're on an errand?" He nodded to the folded paper she held.

Ellanor turned the invitation to hide the name written on it.

"Let's walk together," he said.

"Please do not inconvenience yourself, my lord. If you'll give me leave . . ."

"Nonsense, Mistress Fitzhugh. Your company is extremely diverting. Indeed, I shall walk with you."

Ellanor could not refuse, "As you wish my lord." Out of the corner of her eye she saw Priscilla's warning glance. Ellanor gave a quick shake of her head before continuing down the passageway. Priscilla took her place behind her mistress.

"You have seen our beautiful Queen?" asked Lord Wetherby. "Her gracious character and love of conversation lead me to assume she has spoken with you."

"She has been most condescending, but I am hardly worthy of her attention."

"You do yourself a disservice. Nonetheless, I can only imagine that any conversation with Her Majesty is both amusing and delightful," he glanced at Ellanor, "is it not?"

"Indeed, what little I've heard has been both. I'm frequently on errands as you see me now." Ellanor pushed the paper further into the folds of her skirt.

A look of annoyance crossed Lord Wetherby's face. He began again. "Her Majesty holds Lady Carlisle in the highest regard."

"I believe she does, my lord."

"Has she mentioned when Her Majesty will be leaving for Wellingborough?"

"Lady Carlisle has not told me of the Queen's plans, my lord."

"Surely Lady Carlisle knows where the Queen will spend the summer. Her Majesty so enjoys Wellingborough. She often takes the waters there."

"I didn't know."

"Hmmm. I was unable to attend her ladyship's entertainment last week. Tell me, who was there that I shall regret having missed?"

Ellanor grimaced just a little. "My lord, my time was consumed by young noblemen all seeking to press me into conversation. I saw very little else, I assure you."

The expression on Lord Wetherby's face became a smirk. "Ah, yes. I'd quite forgot. You're here to marry a title. I assure you, the Court is watching and wishes you good hunting. Isn't Lord Saxby's whelp among the pack? Now that's a family for a country girl like yourself."

Ellanor clamped her jaw shut and stared at the floor ahead of her. She felt her face growing hot and knew she was blushing.

Lord Wetherby laughed. "May I assume Lord Netherfield attended?"

Ellanor wanted to tell Lord Wetherby he could assume anything he desired. Instead she said, "Aside from those with whom I spoke, I couldn't be certain who attended." She turned a corner, but Lord Wetherby never missed a step.

He shifted to a new line of conversation. "I know that Mr. Pym is in London. He and Lady Carlisle frequently enjoy supper together."

"Really, my lord?"

"He leads the opposition in His Majesty's government. What do you think of his ideas?"

"I have seen him only twice. He didn't speak to me."

"It pains me to hear of some of his charges against the King."

"My lord?"

"This is an unsettled time, I fear."

"It is?"

Lord Wetherby took Ellanor by the elbow and pulled her to a stop. When he spoke, his voice was no longer kind. "I am not accustomed to pert answers from anyone, much less from a common chit. You'll answer the questions I put to you."

"My lord? Which questions have I not acknowledged? Indeed, I have responded to each of your questions. If I cannot give the answers you wish, it is because I do not know them." Ellanor saw Priscilla take two steps toward Lord Wetherby. Her hands were clenched into fists, ready for action.

"My lord, I must complete my errand," Ellanor said.

Lord Wetherby released her and stood back. "I quite forgot to whom I was speaking, my friend from the rose garden in Bath. I hope you'll overlook my pointed questioning. After all, it is the King I protect." His smile did not reach his eyes. "Pardon me, but I have not seen your letter for some moments. You haven't dropped it, have you? No? Then I shall carry it for safekeeping."

Ellanor held the message tighter. The stiff paper crumpled between her fingers.

He held out his hand.

Priscilla edged closer.

"Ah, my lord. At last, I've found you." A young man about Ellanor's age bowed before Lord Wetherby.

"Yes?" His lordship's eyes flickered at the interruption. "Excuse me, please." He lowered his hand and took the messenger aside.

When he returned, he glanced toward the folded paper still hidden in Ellanor's skirts. "My presence is required elsewhere. I hope we shall meet again when you are more at leisure." There was no warmth in his voice. He turned and was gone.

The messenger waited until Lord Wetherby's footsteps no longer echoed in the hallway before he spoke. "His lordship," he smiled broadly, "gets a bit above himself, he does. I hope my interruption annoyed him. . . . Oh, sorry." He swept a deep bow. "Roland Stuart, that's s-t-u-a-r-t, Scots spelling, at your service." When he straightened, his brown hair fell over his forehead and nearly hid his eyes. "I've not seen you at the palace before."

Ellanor ignored his last comment and curtsied. "Well, Roland Stuart, Scots spelling," she said, "you intervened at the best possible moment. Thank you. Now I, too, must be on my way. Priscilla?"

"Mind how you go," Roland called after them.

Ellanor's hands trembled. Her knees wobbled as she walked away.

"What's your name?" he called again.

Ellanor was afraid her voice would shake if she spoke again. It was Priscilla who turned and waved before hurrying after her mistress.

That evening Ellanor told Lady Carlisle of their meeting with Lord Wetherby.

"Please, tell me all you remember, my dear."

Ellanor repeated as much of the conversation as she could.

"It must have been a frightening experience."

"It might have been," said Priscilla, "but my mistress followed your instructions to the letter. She answered every question without saying anything and was polite all the time." She turned to Ellanor, "Did you see the state of the invitation when you handed it over to Lady Mountjoy? You'd clutched it so hard, it looked like you'd thrown it under the wheels of a coach." Priscilla laughed. "Sorry, Lady Carlisle, but it was funny."

Ellanor started to laugh. "Then you came creeping up behind him. . . . The look on your face, your hands in fists. Well, Lord Wetherby is fortunate that the messenger arrived when he did!"

Lady Carlisle's smile grew to a chuckle and ended in a most unladylike laugh. She dabbed at her eyes with her handkerchief. "How I wish I'd been there . . . To see the Commander of the King's Guard baffled by two girls . . . Oh dear, I can't catch my breath!"

CHAPTER FIFTEEN

ON SPYING

"Limbourne!" Lord Wetherby pushed past the servant leading him to Lord Limbourne's private chambers. He burst through the door without knocking. "George!"

Lord Limbourne bustled in from his dressing room. His man-servant was still brushing the back of his coat. "Be gone, be gone," his master said and shooed the servant away. He turned to his guest. "You've finally returned to London, and not a moment too soon. Parliament has the bit between its teeth. Soon we'll have no monarch at all—but I see you are in a mood."

"Mood! You don't know the half!" Lord Wetherby spoke through clenched teeth.

"Edmund, please calm yourself! You'll have me in a state of exhaustion. Let's go into my sitting room." Lord Limbourne led his guest to a small parlor and rang for a servant.

Lord Wetherby stepped in front of his host. "I don't want refreshments!" He threw himself into a chair.

"Nevertheless . . ." Lord Limbourne gave a servant instructions for a generous tray before he sat down. "Now, what gives me the pleasure of your company?"

"George," Lord Wetherby fought to control his voice, "can Lady Wilthrop make any connection between you and me regarding the placing of Ellanor?"

"I assure you, though Lady Wilthrop sings the girl's praises and continues to thank me for advising her of the position with Lady Carlisle, I say nothing." Lord Limbourne's voice quavered a bit.

"You'd better be telling the truth. Something or someone set that girl on her guard. I'll swear to it. If I discover it was you . . ." He paused. When he spoke again, his voice was quiet. "I will discover where the heart of the treason lies and who the leaders are. Anyone who helps them even in ignorance will find himself on a quick journey to the gallows."

"Dear me, as bad as that?" Lord Limbourne licked his lips.

Lord Wetherby's expression silenced his host. "When I met her quite by chance this morning, I couldn't drag anything but two-word sentences past her teeth. She couldn't have done better at saying nothing if I'd trained her myself." Lord Wetherby brought his fist down on the small table beside his chair. A porcelain figurine rocked.

"Edmund!" Lord Limbourne caught the priceless treasure as it toppled and set it back in its place. "Perhaps she was simply over-awed by your presence."

Lord Wetherby looked at his host. "Have you heard nothing?" He bit the syllables out evenly. "Someone has surely warned her. She said nothing, and she was carrying a letter from Lady Carlisle to someone in the palace! I nearly had it!"

"What stopped you?"

"That Stuart boy came with a message for me."

"Who? Oh, the King's nephew . . . hmmm. Let me think, related through His Majesty's sister?" He shook his head. "No, His Majesty's br—?"

Lord Wetherby's glare snapped Lord Limbourne back to the present. "My best plans, so long putting them in place . . . they're coming to nothing."

A servant appeared with a tray of cakes, cups and saucers, and two steaming pots, one of coffee and one of milk. The men sat quietly until the door latch clicked shut behind him.

"Coffee's very soothing to the nerves, I find." Lord Limbourne himself poured for his friend and passed the steaming cup to him. "Sugar's just here. Edmund, surely all is not lost. Perhaps the girl can tell you nothing about Lady Carlisle. But what about pushing the girl and Lord Netherfield together? Something could yet come of that."

Lord Wetherby took a sip before he spoke. "The friendship is going well by all accounts. My sources tell me they were both at Lady Esancy's estate during Christmas."

"Well, that's something."

"It might have been, but they've seldom met since then. He's been much too busy supporting that traitor Pym, who's tearing apart the monarchy. Did you know John's become Pym's private secretary? Oh, yes." Lord Wetherby nodded and took another sip of coffee. "The girl sees little of John and won't say a word about Lucy." He furrowed his brow.

"You've come to a full stop, then, with regard to the girl?"

"For now. My sp—people say—well, that's no matter."

"Women, a man just can't depend on 'em," Lord Limbourne said. He helped himself to a small cake.

Lord Wetherby finished his coffee in silence. As he put his cup and saucer down, a slow smile appeared on his face. "I don't know about coffee settling one's nerves, but it appears to be good for the mind. I have another idea or two." He rose, bowed to his host, and strode from the room. The door slammed behind him.

"Oh, dear me." Lord Limbourne drew a hand across his forehead. "I'd rather have him shouting than quiet. . . . Much more dangerous in his quiet mood, yes. . . . I did my part, though, and did it well. Why should he blame me if his plans go awry? Serve my King, that's what he said. Do this one thing for me, and I did." Lord Limbourne pushed himself out of his chair and paced the length of his sitting room twice.

CHAPTER SIXTEEN

OATLANDS

On August 12, King Charles and Lord Wetherby left London to open Parliament in Scotland. Barely two weeks later, the Queen's mother ended her visit and returned to the continent. When, later that month, both plague and smallpox struck the City, the Queen removed her family to Oatlands, the royal estate in Surrey.

Lady Carlisle followed and took chambers at an inn in the nearby village of Walton on Thames. The innkeeper greeted her as an honored guest who always spoke for his best rooms and paid her bills on time. This summer he was even more delighted when she engaged two extra chambers for her young companion.

Her ladyship spent long hours with the Queen consoling her on the absence of her husband. A few days later messengers from Parliament arrived demanding that Prince Charles continue his studies at Richmond. The Ministers of Parliament feared that the Queen would instruct England's next king in Roman Catholicism. The Queen demanded even more of Lady Carlisle's sympathy and comfort.

Ellanor spent her few free hours with Priscilla exploring the royal estate and surrounding villages. She wrote to her family about her duties, the beauty of Oatlands, and how each evening, after Her

Majesty went in to supper, she and Lady Carlisle walked down the long avenue from the Queen's residence. At the end of the avenue grew the cedar tree planted barely a year before by King Charles to commemorate the birth of his third son. Prince Henry of Oatlands had died shortly after.

Ellanor's father responded, noting that on two occasions her letters had been tampered with before he received them. Some curious post-boy, no doubt, he said, but it was annoying when a father and daughter could not exchange letters without someone else reading them first. Priscilla's parents said her letters also were opened before they arrived home.

Other refugees from plague-ridden London arrived at Oatlands. Lady Wilthrop arrived in late August. Lady Esancy and Lord Netherfield arrived two days later. Mr. Pym came in the dark of night early in September and took a late supper at Lady Carlisle's inn. Until the rising of the sun he met with her ladyship and Lord Netherfield. When Mr. Pym left, the Earl of Netherfield accompanied him.

September passed quietly. The politics of Parliament were thirty miles away, and the King and Lord Wetherby remained in Scotland. Neither plague nor smallpox afflicted the countryside. Farmers harvested their late crops and gave thanks that there would be no hunger during the coming winter. The recently harvested fields smelled rich and earthy in the warm sun.

Harvest festivals created a brisk business for traveling minstrels, jugglers, actors, and acrobats. Lady Carlisle and Lady Wilthrop shooed the girls to the celebration in Walton on Thames. Ellanor and Priscilla strolled among the booths that sold sweets, ribbons, and trinkets. They stopped to watch the morris dancers and gave the Fool six pence when he came through the crowd.

"Mistress!" Priscilla was straining to see over the people in front of her. "I'm sure I just saw Lord Netherfield. He must have returned from London."

Ellanor looked in the same direction as her maid. "Where? I don't see him."

"Over there." Priscilla nodded. She had heard that pointing was considered rustic and kept her hands clasped at her waist.

"I still don't see him. Anyway, in this crowd, I doubt our paths will cross."

Nevertheless, in fewer than ten minutes Lord Netherfield greeted them. "Mistress Ellanor, isn't this a glorious day? The sun is shining, and look at the blue of the sky." He pulled Ellanor's arm through the crook of his elbow. "Let's get away from the crowd. I have news!"

They walked to a quiet place by the river.

"How good to see you again, Lord Netherfield. We missed you after you returned to London. May I say that you look like the cat that ate the cream?"

"I feel like that selfsame cat. That's why I've returned to Oatlands, to share news of my good fortune with Aunt Esancy and . . . with you."

"My lord?"

"You know that my family is land rich and money poor."

Ellanor nodded.

"On Lady Day last, two of my tenants renewed their leases. The leases had been for three lives, but . . . that's not important." Lord Netherfield waved the trivia away. "What is important is that these tenants had done quite well and were willing to pay large fines and higher rents to renew."

"That's wonderful—"

"Ah, but the best is yet to come." Lord Netherfield lowered his voice. "I took the advice of Lady Wilthrop. Invested it all in a trading venture to the Mediterranean. The ship returned ten days ago, and the profits were above expectations."

"That *is* good news."

Priscilla said, "I wish you all good fortune, my lord."

"Thank you, Priscilla. Master Perry certainly knows his business. Shrewd but honest, that's what Lady Wilthrop said. Yes, she put me on to him. Buys her coffee and tea directly from him. It seems her husband and the Perry family knew each other well."

"And you've been sitting in London counting your profits?"

"Indeed, yes. I could shout this from the rooftops, but you know how most of the nobility frown on commerce. The relief I feel! I wish father could enjoy this as well, but he no longer knows one day from another." Lord Netherfield shook his head, then quickly smiled. "Still, having more than two coins to rub together is so . . ." He struggled for the right word.

Ellanor laughed. "And will you continue investing? If Father were here, he'd advise you so."

"Master Fitzhugh's advice would be welcome. He's one of the most successful merchants in the West Country." He squared his shoulders and looked out across the river. "It makes a man feel worthwhile, somehow. If good fortune continues, I shall soon have no need to marry an heiress."

"You'll be able to marry for advantage, then."

"Yes, I shall." Lord Netherfield paused. "I'm sorry to take my leave, Mistress Ellanor. I must see Aunt Esancy and share my good news with her."

He bowed over her hand, then hurried off through the crowd.

Priscilla moved to her mistress's side. "Does this mean you won't marry Lord Netherfield?"

"Marry Lord Netherfield?" Ellanor thought for a moment. "I don't think there ever was much chance of that. And now that he's recovering his family's fortune, there will be many noble families wishing to ally themselves with the house of Netherfield."

"Aren't you sorry?"

"There's such a difference in our ages. Besides, we agreed to a pact of friendship last Christmas."

"Yes, but are you sorry he won't need to marry an heiress . . . like you? I quite like him."

Ellanor's long sigh sounded as if it started from her toes. "It looks as if I'll marry someone like Lord Saxby's son. Thank goodness they didn't come to Oatlands."

LADIES

The Ladies Wilthrop and Carlisle frequently complimented themselves and each other on the progress of Ellanor and Priscilla. Today they sat in one of Oatlands' gardens taking a cup of tea.

"Could their parents see them," said Lady Carlisle to her friend, "they would not recognize their daughters. They are no longer girls, Mary, but graceful young women walking through the gardens and across the lawns of a royal estate as though born to it."

"Ellanor is much too cordial with her maid," opined Lady Wilthrop. "See how they walk, arm in arm, more like sisters than mistress and maid. I've spoken with her regarding that." She stirred a spoonful of sugar into her tea.

"Every woman must have a confidant." Lady Carlisle spoke with the certainty of one who had suffered the attacks of enemies.

They watched the young women talking quietly and gesturing calmly as ladies of good breeding should. Both gathered their shawls more closely about their shoulders in the cool breezes of early autumn.

"They are but fifteen years of age," Lady Wilthrop responded. "Nevertheless, they have become accomplished young ladies."

"Indeed," came the reply, "Ellanor is fit to marry into the nobility at any time. Perhaps Lord Saxby's son, Sir Henry?"

Lady Wilthrop wrinkled her nose in distaste. "I had hoped for better, perhaps even Lord Netherfield, but their acquaintance has never gone beyond friendship. At least I can tell her parents there is one serious suitor."

Lady Wilthrop's letters assured the Master and Mistress of Bishop's Manor that Ellanor would repay their investment of love and treasure many times over. This winter's season, she wrote, will polish all that thus far has been accomplished. Yes, there is one serious suitor. Sir Henry Willingham, the next Earl of Saxby, has bowed over Ellanor's hand on several occasions. At least the young nobleman's father is serious. One must also mention Lord Netherfield, grand nephew of Lady Esancy. He appears to have a genuine regard for Ellanor. There is, however, no rush; she will be but sixteen in November. And, yes, Priscilla is doing well.

Master and Mistress Fitzhugh read and reread the letters and smiled at their daughter's success. The Fitzhughs called on Priscilla's parents and celebrated the news with a dinner of five courses that lasted for two hours. Even so, it was difficult for the two sets of parents to accept they would not see their daughters for another winter. "It's a trial to be borne," said Mistress Fitzhugh to Priscilla's mother.

"Oh, yes," came the answer. "I don't know where I'd put Priscilla if she did come home, our house is just that full."

October blustered into November. The days grew shorter, and the winds blew colder. The pace of life in the countryside slowed as farmers gathered their lives closer to their cottage hearths. Crops were stored, the last animals slaughtered, sausages and cheeses made. Work moved from the fields to the barns. The wheeze of bellows and hammering of iron told of the mending of harness, ploughs, and carts. And everyday the sound of axe on wood signaled that this autumn was already colder than any of recent memory.

The frosts brought an end to the plague and smallpox in London, and the Queen returned to Whitehall. By early November, Walton on Thames was a quiet country village once again.

Barely had Lady Carlisle's servants unpacked when the news arrived of rebellion in Ireland. The Irish had slaughtered hundreds of Englishmen. Those who could, fled, many with only the clothes they wore. By the time they arrived in England, they looked more like beggars than peers of the realm.

Members of the House of Commons rose, one by one, to denounce this new conspiracy between the Queen and her Roman Catholic friends. Public outcry, which had died down during Her Majesty's summer at Oatlands, rose once again to a fever pitch. Charles, still in Scotland, heard of the rebellion while he was playing golf on the links at Leith. He left immediately for London. The Queen hurried north to the royal estate of Theobalds to meet him.

"There's no reason for you to journey to Theobalds. I, however, have no choice." Lady Carlisle's tone was exasperated. She held in her hand the card that had been delivered only moments before to summon her to the Queen's side. "I doubt I shall be gone more than ten days. In fact, it will give you an opportunity to learn how to manage a large household."

She held up her hand at Ellanor's protest. "The housekeeper will give you every help. Invite Lady Wilthrop for supper. Redecorate your apartments. Get rid of the gray hangings. They never suited you. Most important, keep the seamstresses busy on our gowns. They must be ready as soon as the Court returns to London. The City will celebrate the King's return, even if they don't care for him."

Lady Carlisle leaned forward to kiss Ellanor's cheek. She whispered, "Beware the maid, Lilian."

"Why don't you send her away?" Ellanor asked. Lilian had been found in parts of the mansion where she had no duties.

Lady Carlisle and Ellanor walked down the hall to the heavy wooden entry doors. "If I discharge her, Wetherby will know I've discovered one of his tools."

Ellanor raised both eyebrows in surprise. "You know?"

Lady Carlisle nodded. "Oh, yes, she's his. Only recently, a friend at Court repeated to me the contents of a letter I'd written and left on my desk. I watched Lilian enter the room after I left."

"It sounds as though you hid and waited for her."

"I did. Can you imagine? Me, a spy in my own house. Only she could have known the letter's contents." The women stepped into the cold winter day.

"Lady Carlisle!" Ellanor laughed. "I had no idea you could be so devious. I hope no harm was done by her seeing the letter."

"None. There wasn't a word of truth in it! The problem is, there may be others helping her. At least, knowing about Lilian, I can control some of the information that may be passed along."

Lady Carlisle settled into the coach. She gave a last wave as Ellanor stepped back into the mansion.

Mr. Pym called the next afternoon. Ellanor asked him, as a friend of Lady Carlisle's, to join her and Lady Wilthrop for supper.

The leader of the House of Commons bowed. "It will be a pleasure."

After dessert, Ellanor dismissed the servants.

Lady Wilthrop said, "I hope you don't mind answering a political question, sir."

"Not at all." Mr. Pym bowed to her across the table.

"I've heard," she said, "that the Queen is held responsible for the late rebellion in Ireland. Can this be true?"

Mr. Pym propped his elbows on the table. He held his cup with both hands and tipped the coffee into his mouth. He rolled it on his tongue as if it were a fine wine before swallowing. "I believe I can give you an answer. Though, for the moment, I ask you not to repeat what I say."

Lady Wilthrop and Ellanor nodded.

"The Commons knows that Her Majesty has long protected Roman Catholics from our courts. She has also contacted them for money." He paused. "Many believe that some of those funds reached the leaders of the rebellion."

"She encouraged the rebellion?" Disbelief registered in every word of Ellanor's question.

"How else would the Irish dare burn homes and fields, slaughter cattle, and massacre at least five thousand Englishmen unless they were assured of the Queen's support and protection?"

"Five thousand? How dreadful. We heard several hundred. A large enough number to be sure." Lady Wilthrop's voice was a whisper. "Have you proof?"

"A Parliamentary committee sought out the truth of the matter."

"I've served at Court for a almost a year," said Ellanor. "The Queen has suffered much, yet I've never seen her strike out in anger."

They sat quietly for several moments.

Mr. Pym broke the silence. "I assure you, it is so." He leaned back in his chair and spoke in a more normal tone. "But, see here, government is not always so serious. Let me leave you with a more cheerful story."

"Please do," said Lady Wilthrop.

"Sometimes," said Mr. Pym, "I believe schoolboys conduct themselves with more decorum than do the honorable members of Parliament. Only a few days ago one of our debates became so heated that the ministers shouted and banged their sword scabbards on the floor to drown out the speakers."

Lady Wilthrop looked at Mr. Pym as if he were a little boy caught telling a lie.

"Then," said Mr. Pym, "and I do not exaggerate, they went to brawling and pulling on each other's wigs. Some went flying the length of the Chamber. It looked more like a wrestling match than a meeting of the august members of Commons."

"I wish I'd been in the gallery," said Ellanor. "That would be something to tell Father."

"Something to see, it really was." Mr. Pym chuckled.

"Of course, Mr. Pym," said Lady Wilthrop, "you were not involved."

"Me? No, no. Not that I wouldn't have liked to punch a nose or two." He pushed back his chair and rose. "Now I must take my leave and return to that same dignified body."

CHAPTER 17 Exchange

The servant Lilian hurried from the door and into the shadows of the servants' passageway. Nothing! Nothing, again! She'd been able to hear nothing of the conversation in the dining room except for the story of the fisticuffs on the Commons floor. Lord Wetherby would not be pleased.

THREATS

The Lord Mayor and Aldermen of London, attended by five hundred horsemen, rode out to Theobalds to greet King Charles. Heavy rain forced them to spend the night under a great tent. The next morning it was a damp embassy that bowed before the royal presence. The Recorder of London stepped forward and said, "I can truly say this from the representative body of your City. They meet Your Majesty with as much love and affection as ever citizens of London met with any of your royal progenitors." With that they invited His Highness to a celebration in the City and a banquet in the Guildhall.

Lady Carlisle wrote a hurried note to Ellanor. "We shall attend the banquet. The seamstress must finish a gown for each of us. Double her fees! Given what I already pay her, she'll soon be able to retire to her own country estate."

On November 25, the royal family reached London. The King and the Prince of Wales rode their favorite horses. Queen Henrietta Maria and the younger princes and princesses rode in closed coaches. The Commander of the King's Guard set his men around their majesties, sent his spies among the merrymakers, then took his place in the procession. He pulled his cloak close against the cold.

The King entered the City at Moorgate. Londoners cheered. Kitchen wenches and apprentices danced in the streets. Merchants and beggars elbowed each other in the crowd. Musicians played, trumpets sounded, and the conduits in Cornhill and Cheapside flowed with claret.

At the Guildhall, Lord Wetherby reined his horse in at the east end of the square. His horse shifted under him when a drunken apprentice stumbled against the animal. His lordship cursed and swung his whip across the back of the offender. The young man howled and staggered away supported by a boy as unsteady as his friend.

Lord Wetherby surveyed the growing throng. How quickly a celebration might become a riot. He nodded to one of his guards and raised his hand in greeting to an acquaintance. Only when he saw familiar faces did the Captain of the Guard rein his mount across the square.

Lady Wilthrop, Ellanor, Martha, and Priscilla stood near the church wall of St. Lawrence Jewry. "This is about the best we can do, I think," said Lady Wilthrop. "We're out of the wind and not being pushed about too much. I had no idea so many would be here."

"Surely, not all these people are waiting for the banquet." Ellanor stepped closer to the church wall to let a guardsman pass.

"Definitely not. It's by invitation only." Lady Wilthrop patted her pocket. "I have our cards. The excitement is—Oh! There's Lady Montague." She waved to her friend. "Ellanor, I'll return presently." Lady Wilthrop disappeared into the press of people. Martha followed elbowing bystanders out of her way.

The Captain of the Guard dismounted and tossed his horse's reins to a guardsman. "Mistress Fitzhugh, is it not?" His bow was nearly nonexistent.

"My lord." Ellanor curtsied.

"Did I not see Lady Wilthrop?"

"She has stepped away for a moment."

"And Lady Carlisle?"

"Is waiting on the Queen, my lord."

"Her devotion to Her Majesty is commendable." There was no approval in his voice. "In truth, I wish to speak with you . . . away from the crowd." Lord Wetherby grasped Ellanor's arm and propelled her across the square toward the entrance of the Guildhall.

Priscilla struggled to keep up.

"My lord, I must protest." Ellanor tried to free her arm. "Lady Wilthrop will not know where to find me when she returns."

Lord Wetherby's grip tightened. "I'll send a messenger to her when I've finished." He pulled Ellanor through the Guildhall entrance and into a small chamber. "This will do." He closed the hangings that served as the door. The walls were hung with heavy red velvet. The fire burning in the small fireplace gave the room a cheerful glow. The flames of three candles on the table waved and flickered in drafts from the doorway.

A moment later Priscilla pulled the heavy drapery aside. She saw her mistress, rubbing her arm, standing before Lord Wetherby. He had perched on the edge of a table. He held his left arm across his body to support his right elbow. His chin rested on his right thumb and fingers. His expression reminded Priscilla of pictures she'd seen of a wolf regarding its next meal. There was no one else in the room. She hesitated only a moment then whirled and ran.

Ellanor had not seen Lord Wetherby since June when the Queen's Court left for Oatlands. After returning to Whitehall in October, she and Priscilla had avoided his lordship. Now she stood before him alone, with no escape possible.

"Enjoying London, Mistress Fitzhugh?"

"My lord?"

He chuckled as though at a joke. "And husband hunting, that's been good? I hear the house of Saxby is ripe and ready to fall into your . . . or should I say your father's . . . lap." Lord Wetherby flicked an imaginary speck of dust from his sleeve. "Surely you can do better."

Ellanor said nothing. She'd heard enough comments about her errand in London to be able to ignore them.

Lord Wetherby shrugged. "I thought a few pleasantries . . . but, you do not answer. Very well, I'll move directly to the reason for our meeting. You can't elude me this evening. You'll hear me and fulfill your purpose."

Ellanor's mind snapped to attention.

"Did you think it was by chance that I spoke to you that day at Bath?" he continued. "You were even then part of a well-considered plan. To set it in motion, I needed someone whom no one in London knew. When I learned that Lady Wilthrop was bringing another girl to London, I set out for Bath. She always stops there, you know. We met, and I was sure you were exactly the right girl to serve my purpose, naive and easily impressed though a trifle too inquisitive."

Ellanor was embarrassed at how accurate his impression had been of her.

"I must admit it was more difficult introducing you into Lady Carlisle's household. That took longer than I'd hoped."

Ellanor did not move, but her eyes opened wider.

"That surprised you, I see. It was done rather well if I do say so." His smile faded. "Not all went as planned, however. You were told not to speak to me? By whom?"

Ellanor's mouth was dry. She had to swallow before she could speak. "In fact, my lord, your position at Court kept me from any familiarity."

His lordship dismissed her comment with a wave of his hand. "Who warned you against me?"

Ellanor hesitated. This man had the power to arrest anyone she might name! "No one warned me. . . . It was my decision, entirely my own, especially after you tried to take the letter from me. You frightened me, my lord."

"I see." Lord Wetherby leaned toward her. "I brought you to London to serve your King."

Ellanor wanted desperately to move so the table was between them. Instead she stood her ground and said, "Lady Wilthrop brought me to London, my lord, to fulfill my father's wishes."

"You forget your place." Lord Wetherby's voice was a sneer. "During your weeks among the nobility, you have adopted airs that do not become the daughter of a common merchant."

"There is nothing common about my father, my lord."

His lordship walked to the fireplace and stood silently for a moment. When next he spoke it was with his full authority as Commander of the Guard. "You will obey me. Lady Carlisle is a spy for John Pym, that traitor who would remove our King altogether. I know that she passes whatever the Queen says directly to him. I lack only the means to prove it. You will provide that proof so I can arrest her and all her household right down to the rats in her cellars . . . in spite of Her Majesty," he added under his breath,

Ellanor gasped, "I?" The room around her seemed to disappear. She no longer felt the table that held her up. She did not hear the people passing outside the chamber or see the fire burning on the hearth. She heard and saw only the man who threatened Lady Carlisle. After many seconds she remembered to breathe.

"That's a relief," said Lord Wetherby. "For a moment I thought you might faint. Funny how women are able do that at will." He shook his head as if mystified. "But there's no need for that. It's quite simple, really. You speak with Lady Carlisle nearly every day. All I want is to know what her ladyship says to you. It will all be done quietly. She need never know."

Ellanor looked at the man before her as though seeing a mythic beast for the first time.

A threat entered his voice. "The question of treason might even extend to you, Mistress Fitzhugh. You also have entertained Mr. Pym at supper on at least one occasion. And, as you know, whole families can be destroyed by the actions of one." He gestured to the building around them. "Many have been tried and condemned in this very hall."

Ellanor forced her lips to move. "Family?"

"Whether or not your father loses all that he has, perhaps even his life, is in your hand. You can condemn him or win him honor. I'm sure you'll wish to take advantage of the opportunity I present to you."

"Opportunity?"

"Consider—" Movement at the door caused him to break off.

CHAPTER 18 Exchange

Priscilla had pulled back the curtain to allow Lady Wilthrop to enter.

Lord Wetherby bowed to Lady Wilthrop. "Ah, Lady Wilthrop, I was hoping you'd discover where I'd brought Mistress Fitzhugh. I could not leave her standing alone in the cold and jostled by the crowd." When he bowed to Ellanor he said, "I hope we'll speak again soon." He turned and left the room.

Lady Wilthrop and Priscilla hurried across the room. "Ellanor, Priscilla said you require my immediate presence, that you were snatched away by Lord Wetherby!" She looked closely at her ward. "You have absolutely no color in your face! Are you feeling ill?"

"Snatched? No . . . no, Lady Wilthrop. It is as he said. Lord Wetherby brought me here as a courtesy." A glance from Ellanor warned Priscilla to silence. "And I'm not ill. . . . Perhaps tired. The crowds, you know." Ellanor allowed herself to be led into the banquet.

CHAPTER NINETEEN

CONFESSION

In the days after the Guildhall banquet Ellanor feared the appearance of either Lord Wetherby or his guards. She jumped at every sound. If anyone other than Lady Wilthrop called at Lady Carlisle's mansion, Ellanor fled to her chambers. She seldom could be coaxed to attend Court and accepted only one Christmas invitation for an evening at Lady Esancy's London home. All other envelopes and cards on the silver tray were answered with regrets.

Neither was Ellanor's mind at rest. She debated constantly with herself. One moment she knew that she must obey Lord Wetherby. He represented King Charles, God's appointed ruler of England. The next, she shuddered at the price of her father's safety, to spy on a woman who had become her friend.

Even if I see Lord Wetherby, I don't have anything to tell him, thought Ellanor. Lady Carlisle has been so busy during Christmas that we've barely said more than two words to each other. What if my silence has caused Lord Wetherby to already declare Father a traitor? It's been nearly a month since I was to contact his lordship! Ellanor's embroidery dropped to her lap. She felt defeated with every thought.

Priscilla honored her mistress's silent request in the Guildhall that she not speak. But she noted that Ellanor ate little and slept less. On the few occasions when Ellanor attended the Queen with Lady Carlisle, Priscilla enlisted Roland's help to ensure that Ellanor never met Lord Wetherby. Even so, Priscilla was certain they were watched, and the feeling followed her home.

One evening when Lady Carlisle was at Court, Lady Wilthrop came and sat with her ward. "What is it, Ellanor, that has carried away your delight in the season?" she asked.

"Perhaps it is the weather that has kept me indoors."

Lady Wilthrop thought Ellanor's smile a bit too bright. It did not ease her worry. "I hope that is the cause." She put her palm on Ellanor's forehead. "You're not ill?"

"Not at all, Lady Wilthrop."

"Lady Carlisle says you've accepted scarcely any invitations and that you have to be entreated, practically begged, to go to Court."

"I visited with Lady Esancy Monday last."

"Well, I'm glad you made the effort to visit her ladyship." Lady Wilthrop sat back in her chair.

"I've gone to Court on occasion. Politics is on everyone's lips. Quite boring, actually. Many families have decided to retire to the country, so the palace is rather quiet." Ellanor looked around the pleasant room. "I've been content to stay here, quiet, warm, and comfortable."

Lady Wilthrop left comforted but not completely convinced that Ellanor was not suffering from some ill humor.

Meanwhile, England's political life grew more turbulent. Parliament charged the King with a long list of abuses and demanded that he mend his ways. There were rumors that an Irish Catholic general and his army were waiting only for a word from the Queen to invade England. The Queen protested with tears that no such alliance existed.

Lord Wetherby would have cornered Ellanor, but he glimpsed her only once as her maid and Roland pushed her around a corner. Well, he'd take care of them soon enough. Just now he was much too busy protecting the King and his talkative wife.

King Charles tried to lessen John Pym's influence in the House of Commons by offering him the Chancellorship of England. Mr. Pym turned his back on the offer. The king then directed his attorney general to draw up articles of treason against Pym and his followers. Parliament refused to turn the accused men over to the Crown.

"Arrest the traitors yourself!" cried the Queen. "Go and pull those rogues out by the ears!"

Under her urging King Charles laid his plans. Only to her and the Commander of the Guard did he reveal that he would personally go to Parliament and seize five of his enemies. On January 5, the day appointed, he hugged the Queen and said, "Only another hour, and I shall be master in my own kingdom."

Henrietta Maria was left counting the minutes and praying for her husband's success. When Lady Carlisle entered her chambers, the Queen, overcome by the tension of waiting, flew to her friend.

"Ah, *ma chère!*" She embraced her lady in waiting.

"Your Majesty, you're agitated! Is there something you require?" Lady Carlisle led the Queen to a chair.

The Queen sat down then bounced back to her feet. "*C'est impossible!* I can't sit down!" Her Majesty caught Lady Carlisle's hands in hers. "Rejoice with me, for at this hour, I pray that the King is master of this country, and that his enemies are without doubt under arrest. . . . But . . . he is late. I should have heard by now."

"What are you saying, Madam? Please, calm yourself. What about the King?"

The Queen whirled away and rushed to the window overlooking the Thames. The river was alive with the business of the City. "*Calme?* How is this possible when soon those horrible little men will go straight to the Tower, and I shall see the King coming in victory?"

"Who will go to the Tower?"

"*Pardon?* Ah, the King's enemies. In the Commons." The Queen crossed the room and shook a finger in the face of her lady in waiting. "One, I believe, you know. That John Pym." She laughed. "You are surprised I know this?"

Lady Carlisle felt a fist tighten around her heart. She hoped her face did not show her fear. "Mr. Pym and I have known each other for many years. That is no secret. But you say the King goes to arrest him?"

The Queen shrugged. "I tell you many are arrested for treason in France."

"Mr. Pym is charged with treason?" Lady Carlisle kept her voice quiet and low.

"*Je ne sais pas.* The charges were drawn up only yesterday. It is enough that his grace, Lord Wetherby, tells my husband that he has proof of Mr. Pym's guilt."

"Wetherby!"

"*Oui.* He persuades my husband, the King, of the necessity of this action. I, also, hurry my dear Charles on his way. Perhaps now he will be able to rule as God intended."

Lady Carlisle's mouth felt as dry as dust. She managed to say, "Yes, we all wish His Majesty well. I . . . I'll have a tray brought to you while you wait." She stepped into the antechamber and sent a servant for wine and sweet biscuits for Her Majesty. Then she gathered her cloak and gloves and left the palace.

The Countess walked up and down while she waited for her coach. She was too anxious to sit down and the movement helped warm her. John hadn't believed the King would move against him for some days. She shook her head. Will His Majesty dare enter the House of Commons? It doesn't matter, she thought. Wetherby will dare. Fortunately, the King's progress towards Parliament will be slow because he stops to listen to every speech and hear every petition. He thinks he's the fountainhead of English justice! That means I have time to warn John.

"My lady! You're leaving early." Someone reined his horse close to her.

Lady Carlisle adjusted her face into a pleasant expression before she looked up. "Ah, my lord. Yes, the Queen is resting."

"Is she? I would have thought she'd be on tenterhooks." Lord Wetherby smiled down at her.

"My lord? Whatever are you saying? Has something happened to Her Majesty?" Lady Carlisle turned toward the palace gate. "I'd better return to her."

Lord Wetherby rode his horse between Lady Carlisle and the gate. His smile broadened. "My lady, I almost believe your apprehension for Her Majesty is genuine. However, I think you'd best continue on your way. And, given these unsettled times, you should not travel through Westminster unescorted. My guardsmen will see you safely home."

"Oh, I was going to—" Lady Carlisle paused, "to my dressmakers. I require no escort."

Lord Wetherby bowed. "Madam, I insist. I could not face Her Majesty if your safety were compromised." He rode away to give the necessary orders.

Once home, Lady Carlisle burst into her parlor. She pulled off her gloves and dropped her cloak from her shoulders. A maid trotted behind to catch her mistress's castoff garments. She curtsied and left the room.

The Countess went straight to the windows that overlooked the bare trees and rain-beaten shrubs of the garden. She stood with her arms crossed over her waist. *Wetherby guessed that the Queen told me everything,* she thought. *And him so smug. I'd like to remove that smirk from his face.* She rubbed the palm of her right hand. *I'll wager he's placed a half dozen guards outside my gate.*

She put her fingertips to her temples. "Think! Think! Think!" she said aloud. Her tone was that of an impatient teacher admonishing a dull-witted student. "The King won't have reached Parliament, yet." She looked up at the ragged clouds, pushed by a cold, wet wind. Raindrops snapped against the window panes. "Even better, the weather will send him to shelter. There's still time!"

"My lady?" Ellanor sat by the fireplace, her embroidery hoop in her hand.

Lady Carlisle whirled around, her hands pressed over her heart. "Ellanor! I didn't see you! . . . You've given me quite a start."

Ellanor stood. "Shall I send one of your maids to you?"

"No. No, thank you. I'm quite all right." She rang for a servant. When he came she asked, "What news from Parliament?"

"None, my lady."

"Bring me any news immediately." She dismissed him.

Ellanor secured her needle in the cloth and put her silk threads in a small basket. She had never before seen the Countess in such a mood. She sat down and waited, not sure whether to stay or go.

A loud pop in the fireplace scattered sparks onto the hearth. It was as if a stopper had been removed from a bottle. Lady Carlisle sat across the hearth and leaned toward Ellanor. "Do you know what he's done? That swine!" A servant appeared to sweep the hearth clean and was himself swept from the room by an abrupt wave of Lady Carlisle's hand.

Ellanor waited for the door latch to click before answering. "Who, my lady? Who did what?"

Lady Carlisle rose, opened each of the doors of the parlor, and peered into the rooms and hallways beyond. Satisfied they were alone, she fastened the latches and returned to her chair. "Lord Wetherby!" Her teeth were clenched and her voice was barely a whisper. "If I were a man, I'd call him to the field of honor and put a ball between his eyes! I would! He's completely despicable." Words failed her.

Ellanor froze. She closed her eyes for a moment to collect her thoughts and make her lips move. "Lord Wetherby?"

"While I waited on the Queen this morning, she told me something I know she should not have." Lady Carlisle stopped, tiptoed again to the nearest door, and pulled it open. Lilian curtsied over a basket of linens before she hurried on her way.

Lady Carlisle hesitated then motioned to another servant in the hallway. "See that Lilian stays in her room for the rest of the day. Tie her to her bed if you must. She may not move until I speak with her.

Go! . . . Now!" She closed the door and returned to her chair. "I've taken all I can from that girl. Where was I?"

Ellanor felt her heart skip a beat. This might be something she could trade for her father's protection! Immediately she felt guilty. "You were waiting on the Queen—"

"Yes, yes. Well, Her Majesty was quite beside herself when I arrived. She told me that the King was on his way to arrest his enemies in Parliament."

"Mr. Pym?"

Lady Carlisle nodded. "And four or five of his closest political allies. The King hates them. These men led Parliament in the impeachment of Strafford and Laud, and everyone knows how His Majesty depended on them. Now Parliament is claiming control of the army and navy. What will come of that, no one knows, but charges of treason have been drawn up against all of them.

"I was on my way to tell John that he must flee, but Lord Wetherby met me. Under the excuse of my safety, his lordship sent four of his guards to escort my coach home. They are probably still in the Strand, watching my door." Lady Carlisle glanced out the garden window. "I hope they're wet to their skin and miserable."

Footsteps passed the door. Both women sat motionless until the hall was quiet.

"Wetherby will accompany the King to Parliament. Someone has to do the actual arresting. The King never could."

"Are you going to warn Mr. Pym?" Ellanor asked.

"I must. I was going to send him a message from the gallery. It would have been so simple."

"If you warn Mr. Pym, aren't you doing just what Lord Wetherby thinks—"

"I would gladly commit treason to save my friend."

"He will arrest you." Ellanor said aloud. To herself she thought, and if I don't tell him what I'm hearing now, he'll ruin Father. If I do tell him, you'll be accused of treason and sent to the block—

"Don't worry about me! I don't stand unprotected." Lady Carlisle reached out and patted Ellanor's hand. "I'll weather this storm—"

"I can't do this." Ellanor's spoke in a whisper.

"Sorry?"

Ellanor sat with her eyes closed. Tears rolled down her cheeks. Her fingers twisted around each other. "Lord Wetherby—" Ellanor collapsed back in her chair.

"Ellanor, you're babbling! Whatever are you saying? No. Wait. I, we need a cup of tea. Actually, we need a large pot of very strong tea." Lady Carlisle rang for a servant. When he left, she listened at the door before returning to her chair by the fire.

Ellanor tried to stifle her sobs.

Lady Carlisle took her hand. "Tell me what has happened. Tell me what Lord Wetherby," Lady Carlisle spat out the name as if it were acid on her tongue, "said to you."

Ellanor wiped her tears away on the back of her free hand and took a long, shaking breath. "I tried to tell you so many times. . . . I was afraid. He threatened to destroy Father. . . . I never told him anything. Now he will arrest me too. He as good as said so at the Guildhall. And Father . . ." She wiped away more tears.

"You're not making much sense, my dear. Can you begin again?"

Ellanor nodded. "The day of the banquet at the Guildhall, Lord Wetherby took me aside and told me there was treason in the Queen's chambers. He said I could serve the King by collecting information from you. That's why he placed me in your household."

Lady Carlisle might have been turned to marble. "He what?"

"That's what he said to me. Lady Carlisle, I never said anything, never! Please, please believe . . ." Ellanor tried to finish the sentence. Her mouth moved, but no words came. She hung her head.

A movement caught Lady Carlisle's attention. A man walked back and forth on a neighboring roof. "A moment, Ellanor," she said and went to the window. The man stared at her for a moment then turned away and disappeared. Lady Carlisle's jaw tightened. She grasped the velvet curtains so firmly to close them that they remained wrinkled when she let go. "He set a spy on the roof overlooking my garden! Guards in the street is one thing, but spying through my windows—!" Lady Carlisle took a small brand from the fire and lit the candles. "So you were to report to Wetherby?" she asked over her shoulder.

Ellanor nodded. "He said that if I didn't tell him all you said, he would ruin Father."

"So that's why you've had to be dragged out of doors these last weeks. I feared you were failing of some illness."

"It's just that he appears so suddenly sometimes. I wish he were at the bottom of the Thames."

"The fish wouldn't have him."

The clatter of china told them of the approach of the servant. Lady Carlisle directed him to set the tray on the table by her chair and dismissed him.

Ellanor went on, "Whenever I went to Whitehall, Priscilla and Roland made sure we never met."

"Roland?" Lady Carlisle asked as she poured hot water on the tea leaves.

"A friend. He's somehow related to the King, but he doesn't act like it." Ellanor hesitated. "What am I going to do now?"

Lady Carlisle covered the pot for the tea to steep. She sat quietly for a few minutes. "I have a certain amount of influence and many friends . . . There are those whom even the Commander of the Guards fears. Messages to the right people . . . I'm sure we can protect your father. Yes, you may put your mind at ease, Ellanor. I shall move today on your father's behalf. I think it quite unlikely Wetherby has moved against your father. The King and Ireland have commanded his full attention these past weeks."

Ellanor slid from her chair to her knees. She grasped Lady Carlisle's hand. "Thank you, my lady! Thank you!"

"Come, now, dry your tears. You will make yourself ill." The Countess leaned over Ellanor and whispered. "All will be made right."

"Will I be arrested?" asked Ellanor.

"Not as long as his lordship believes you may yet serve him." Lady Carlisle frowned and went to the windows. She pulled back the curtains. No one stood on the roof opposite. She let the curtains fall back over the windows. "I can't think. I must have a cup of tea!" She poured their tea and added two spoonfuls of sugar to Ellanor's cup. "Drink this right down. You'll feel better."

Ellanor drank it all. The hot drink helped dissolve her worry and tension. For the first time in days Ellanor took a deep breath that didn't hurt. She wiped her eyes and blew her nose on her serviette.

"Oh, Ellanor!" Lady Carlisle put on a stern face. "The laundry maids will not appreciate that!"

Ellanor looked at her serviette, now a crushed ball of linen. "Perhaps Lilian should be made to wash it."

Lady Carlisle started to laugh, and Ellanor joined her.

"How can we laugh as though we belong in Bedlam when Lord Wetherby threatens us?" Ellanor finally managed to ask.

"I think, if we had not laughed, we would have cried again," said Lady Carlisle. She sipped her tea. "Ummm, burnt my tongue."

"My lady?"

"Hmmm?"

"Was he really responsible for my coming to stay with you?"

"I don't see how. Certainly Lady Wilthrop was unaware of any plans on his part." Lady Carlisle sat straight. "But, enough of this. I still need to get a message to John."

"Mightn't Mr. Pym be under arrest already?"

"I think not. Lord Wetherby was in no hurry to join the King this morning. Now that the weather has turned, His Majesty has, no doubt, taken refuge. Also, I would receive word immediately if the King even attempted to enter the House of Commons."

The crackling of the fire filled the momentary silence.

"Someone in the gallery to send a note to Mr. Pym?" asked Ellanor. "Is that all that's needed? Priscilla and I could do that."

"Oh, no! Lady Wilthrop would have my head for sending you on such an errand! She warned me against letting you get caught up in intrigues at Court. I wonder what she'll say to all this with Wetherby?"

"It would be quite simple, really. I've never attended a debate, and Mr. Pym did invite me. Besides, if it means that Lord Wetherby will be humiliated, . . ." Ellanor's voice shook. "When I think of what he tried to do to my family, and what might happen to Mr. Pym, well, you must let me help."

"Lady Wilthrop would never forgive me. Besides you have been unwell."

"Lady Carlisle, nothing would make me feel more perfectly well than to hear Mr. Pym debate in Parliament."

Her ladyship sat with her head bowed. "Ellanor, I don't deny that what you suggest gives me hope. The King's Guard will keep me from going near St. Stephen's Chapel."

"You can't send a servant if you are unsure about which of your them can be trusted. Think what might happen if you sent a message by one who was loyal to Lord Wetherby."

"I have thought about that. Wetherby's charges against me would be proved, and John would not be warned."

Ellanor poured them each another cup of tea. "Lord Wetherby might let me into Parliament thinking I'd come to report to him."

"No! You must stay away from him. He's a dangerous and powerful man. Do him no favors!"

"Priscilla will go with me."

Lady Carlisle bit her lower lip. "It might work. If the guards believe you are coming to report to Wetherby—"

"But I wouldn't, of course. I know Whitehall well enough to get to the Chapel without being obvious."

Lady Carlisle sighed. "I can't win this debate with myself. I see it is you who must go. I will write nothing, but Mr. Pym will want proof the message comes from me." She took a gold ring from her finger. "Here, he will recognize this."

Barely ten minutes later a small coach wove its way through carts and carriages in the Strand toward Westminster. Inside, Ellanor and Priscilla pulled their cloaks around them against the cold. The bricks under their feet went cold within minutes.

"Oi! You, there! Stop!" The command came from one of the King's Guard.

"What's this, then?" the coach driver shouted back. "Keeping an honest man from earning his keep?"

"It matters not how honest you are. All the streets to Whitehall are closed to coaches."

"And why would that be?"

"Street's blocked. The King's going to Parliament. Taking his time about it, too, keeping us out in the cold."

"We're not too late!" whispered Priscilla.

The sound of a horse moving beside the coach was followed by the guard's voice. "I'm sorry to say, miss, that the closest you'll get to Whitehall in a coach is right here. You can walk, but I wouldn't advise it. Nasty day."

"So it is," said Ellanor. She allowed herself a slight frown. "You're sure there is no other route? I've been invited by a friend to hear his speech in Parliament this afternoon. . . . He wanted a friendly face in the gallery."

"You can go towards St. James Palace, but that won't get you very close to Whitehall, either."

"I must try. Tell the driver to go to St. James."

"I'd offer an escort, miss, but I've no extra men. Spread that thin, we are." The guard saluted and gave the driver Ellanor's instructions.

Ellanor closed the window and pulled her cloak closer around her. As her coach turned down New Exchange, a third rider joined the guardsmen. "She's going to St. James?" he asked.

"Yes, sir."

The rider turned his horse. "There's no need to follow her any further. I'll tell the Commander where she's going. Keep a sharp eye for any other friends of those rascals in Parliament."

Priscilla blew on her fingers. "Mistress?" she asked. "What if we can't get beyond St. James?"

"I don't know. We'll have to walk, I guess."

"From St. James? In these clothes? Mistress, my hands and feet are nearly frozen."

"Mine, too. At least we can go into the palace to warm ourselves. Perhaps there are coaches going to Parliament from there."

They pulled up outside the brown brick palace of St. James. The driver came to the coach door. "I can take you no farther. We've been turned back. Do you wish to return home?"

Ellanor shook her head.

A footman opened the door and helped Ellanor alight.

"Shall I wait for you, miss?" The driver stood before Ellanor, his cap in his hand. He shivered in the damp wind.

"No. Tell her ladyship we'll try to reach Parliament from here."

CHAPTER 20 Ellanor's Exchange

Ellanor and Priscilla walked quickly into the palace. The grand halls and public chambers were empty except for troops of servants clearing away the clutter left from the holiday celebrations. Ellanor pulled Priscilla toward a fireplace and stretched her hands towards the flames.

"Now what?" asked Priscilla. "It doesn't look as if there's anyone left here who would be going to Whitehall. We're going to have to walk, aren't we?"

Ellanor nodded. "I think so."

Priscilla rubbed her hands together before turning her back to the fire. "We'd better be red hot when we walk out that door," she said.

Ellanor turned to warm her back. "Priscilla, let's find the laundry. We might be able to find extra clothes there."

In the laundry they found heavy woolen clothing worn by the below-stairs maids. Priscilla pulled some garments off the drying racks and handed them to Ellanor. She selected some pieces for herself. "I'm wearing these over my own clothes. Be that much warmer." Her voice was muffled by the heavy woolen shift she was pulling over her head.

Ellanor pulled her shift on. "I don't care what it looks like," she said. "It's warm!" She patted the pocket where she'd put the ring and felt its outline.

Priscilla dived into a pile of folded articles. She held a jumper and a pair of woolen stockings out behind her for Ellanor then found some for herself.

Ellanor pulled on the jumper. The sleeves were long enough to cover her hands. She held up the stockings. "Can we get our shoes on over these?"

"Most definitely," said Priscilla. She sat down on a bench and began pulling them on. "They're thick and warm. I'll make my shoes fit."

"Move over." Ellanor sat down and followed her maid's example. "I have so many layers on, I can barely bend in the middle."

"Caps, caps, caps, where would they be? Aha!" Priscilla appropriated two caps. "Your hat, madam." She bowed to Ellanor. "Capes

126

and scarves are on the pegs by the door. We'll have to leave our own behind. They're much too fine for maids."

"So hats are back this winter." Ellanor tucked her hair under the floppy cap. "Ready? Now, how do we get out of here?"

Priscilla opened the door just far enough to check that no one was in the corridor. They pulled their caps down over their foreheads, looked down at the floor, and hurried up the steps toward the main door of the palace. "Mistress, all of your hair isn't cov—"

"You . . . maids. Stop!"

"It's Roland!" Priscilla whispered.

"What's he doing here? We can't stop for him."

"Is it customary for cleaning wenches not to answer a member of the Court?" A deeper voice asked. Ellanor and Priscilla could see the boots of the man who spoke to them.

The girls gave quick curtsies. "Yes, . . . no my lord," said Priscilla in a squeaky voice. Ellanor had a fit of coughing.

Roland stepped forward and bowed so deeply to Lord Wetherby that the feather in his cap swept the floor. "I thank you my lord," he said, "for stopping these two wenches. I have errands for them."

Lord Wetherby glared Roland to silence. He turned to the girls. "I haven't time for this." He hurried away.

Roland turned to the girls. "I say, you're quiet. Who are you? You'd better answer. Look up!"

"Yes, my lord." Ellanor coughed again.

"Mistress Ellanor? What are you doing in those clothes? Tell me—"

"Shhhhh! We'll be gone immediately and leave you to yourself."

Roland hesitated for only a moment. "Follow me." He led them past the kitchens and laundry into the storage cellars. There he pushed open a heavy wooden door and stepped through. He lit a candle and stuck it on a box. "No one will bother us here. What's going on? Why are you two dressed like this?"

"What was Lord Wetherby doing here? Why isn't he with the King? If he'd recognized us . . ." Ellanor left the sentence unfinished.

"Priscilla! He isn't with the King! Surely he would be, if the King had reached Parliament. We still have time!"

"He's probably checking the guards he left here; he trusts no one. Time for what?" Roland stood with his arms folded across his chest.

"We can't tell you." Ellanor said. "Please show us the way out of here."

"Are you running away?"

"Running away?" Priscilla stamped her foot. "Don't be daft. Would we run away into a palace? We've important business and must be on our way."

"Dressed like that?"

"Yes."

"What is it? Is it secret?"

"If we told you," Ellanor said, "it wouldn't be secret, would it?"

"I just saved you from Lord Wetherby, again. You should be grateful."

"We are, believe me, but we must be on our way." Ellanor looked around the room. "What's the quickest way out of here?"

"Please, Roland." Priscilla grabbed his arm. "It's a matter of—"

"Life and death?" Roland grinned. "You need me. You'll never get out of here without me. These cellars go on forever. Tell me what you're doing. Let go my arm." Roland shook himself free of Priscilla's grasp.

Ellanor started for the door. "If you won't show us the way out, we'll find it ourselves."

"Not easily. Tell me what's going on. I've helped you a lot in the past weeks."

Ellanor pulled her maid behind some boxes for a conference. "Priscilla, we don't know how much time we have. We have to get out of here."

"Maybe he'll help us."

Ellanor stood with her head bent. "We could use a guide. I'm not certain how to get to Whitehall from here."

Ellanor came from behind the boxes.

Roland was waiting. "So?"

"We must deliver a message to one of the ministers of Parliament, and it must be soon. We could use a guide from here to Whitehall."

"You have a message from Lady Carlisle! For John Pym! I'm right, aren't I? Rumor has it she's locked up in her own house."

Ellanor felt her jaw drop open. "How could you kn—She is not locked up!"

"Everyone knows she's been spying for Mr. Pym for years."

"She has not! Lord Wetherby spread those rumors. He's . . . despicable."

Roland perched on the edge of a barrel. "I can get you to Parliament in a few minutes."

"Really? You'll be our guide?"

"If it will annoy Lord Wetherby, sure, I'll guide you. He makes life miserable for me at every opportunity. Besides, there's nothing to do here. Everyone's gone." Roland left his seat on the barrel. "I'll get my cloak. Wait here."

Minutes later Roland reappeared wearing a heavy winter cloak. He wrapped a heavy scarf around his neck and set his hat firmly on his head. "Let's go, then," he said. He picked up the candle, and led the way out of the storeroom. "By the way, I was right about going to see Mr. Pym, wasn't I?"

Ellanor nodded.

Roland led them down one passageway, then another. A smell of damp and mold filled the air. Up stairs and down again, he never paused. Some of the passages were so dark, he paused to light the candle. "Mind your step," he whispered over his shoulder. "Just there . . . and here. Loose stone." He held the candle high so the girls could see.

"What's that squeaking?" Ellanor whispered.

"Rats."

Ellanor put her hand over her mouth to stifle a scream.

Priscilla bumped into her mistress. "Let's get out of here."

Roland turned a corner. "Here we are." He blew out the candle and handed it and his tinderbox to Ellanor before he pushed on the door. "Keep this in one of your pockets, will you? The door doesn't open very far, so you'll have to squeeze through."

"Where are we?" asked Ellanor.

"We've gone the length of the palace underground," said Roland. He led them up a flight of stairs then leaned forward to check the narrow street. Though it was barely five o'clock, the sun had set and the shadows were turning black. When Roland was certain they were alone, he took Ellanor's hand and stepped into the deepest shadows he could find. Ellanor grabbed Priscilla's arm and pulled her along after. To the east they could see a brightly-lit street with its shops.

"Across the park is the shortest way, but it's dangerous in the dark. We'll have to go around."

"Why is it dangerous?" Priscilla asked.

"Likely we'd be robbed." Roland led them toward the busy street.

Between the buildings, Ellanor saw throngs of people, shoulder to shoulder. They must be following the King, she thought. We could never have driven our coach through them.

"This way," said Roland as he dragged her into another alley. Ellanor, in turn, guided Priscilla. The cobbles under their feet were smooth and wet. They slipped and slid with every step.

Roland stopped and said something under his breath. Ellanor and Priscilla ran into him. They stood on the edge of a wide puddle. There was no way to cross without wading through the water.

"Now what?" Priscilla asked.

Roland made a face and waded to the middle. "It's not that deep, just cold."

He walked back to Ellanor. "Hold your skirts," was all he said before he grabbed her around the waist and swung her over the water. He took three steps through the black water and set her down on the other side. Then he waded back and brought Priscilla over in the same way. He stepped out of the water and continued down the alley.

"Oh, his poor, wet feet," said Priscilla.

Ellanor nodded in agreement and ran into Roland's out-stretched arm.

Roland pointed between two buildings to the busy street. "We'll have to walk along the street a ways. There are a lot of guards about. If you don't want to be recognized, try to walk like real cleaning wenches." He reached over and pulled Ellanor's cap down around her face, then did the same for Priscilla. "Pull your hoods up." He stood back and inspected his work. "Slouch a bit more, Ellanor. Stay close to me." He led the way into the street.

Aromas that made Ellanor's mouth water came from some of the shops. She swallowed hard and concentrated on slouching along beside Priscilla. The crowds pushed and jostled them. Elbows dug into Ellanor's back and arms. I'll have bruises no matter how many layers of clothes I have on, she thought.

After what felt like a very long time, they stood outside Whitehall Palace.

Roland pointed, "There's the first gate. We'll cross here and try to get in through the palace gardens." He stepped into the street then jumped back against the wall. He swung his arm to push the girls back against the building.

Lord Wetherby and four mounted guardsmen rode past, scattering the citizens of Westminster right and left. Roland led the girls across the street where they joined hundreds of people all moving toward the gate.

"Oi," Roland hailed a merchant. "What's all this, then?" he asked motioning to the crowds.

"It be the King. Folk heard His Majesty was here, and they're giving him pretty speeches and petitions and such like."

Roland nodded his thanks and led Ellanor through the gate into the Privy Garden.

"I wonder how much longer before the King reaches Parliament?" Ellanor thought out loud.

"If he'd gone directly there, he'd have had time to arrest every minister twice over and throw them all in the Tower," said Roland.

"Maybe he doesn't intend to go to Parliament after all," said Priscilla.

"He still has the arrest warrants, Priscilla." Ellanor held her cloak against the wind. "How long since we left St. James?"

"Not half an hour." Roland led them across the gardens and through a second gate. "We're past the crowds. We can get back on the street again."

They followed him down the road that led to old Westminster Palace where Parliament was sitting.

"See that old gate? It's not used much anymore. Too small for coaches. It goes to the old palace yard."

Ellanor glanced around. "Where's St. Stephen's Chapel? That's where Mr. Pym will be."

"Once we're inside the gate, I'll take you there." Roland took each of the girls by the hand. "Let's go."

CHAPTER TWENTY-ONE

SEARCHERS

Lord Wetherby mounted his horse and led four of his guardsmen from St. James toward Whitehall Palace. He cursed the wind and the cold. He swung his sword at anyone who didn't get out of his way quickly enough.

If only the King had gone directly to Commons, Wetherby thought, this would have been over in less than half an hour. But, no, His Majesty first took refuge from the weather. Now, for two hours and more he's been sitting by the gate, like some know-all judge, listening to dozens of whinging subjects. Move on! Arrest your enemies! Give them the edge of your sword! Or, give me leave to do so. But, no. His Majesty will play the hero for the benefit of his Queen.

Wetherby kicked a man aside. The Queen! His Majesty thinks the sun rises and sets on her. Beautiful, but I'd have sent her back to France within a week. Her tongue never stops wagging. If she were anyone else, she'd have been charged with treason years ago for babbling about affairs of State to anyone and everyone who will listen, including Lady Carlisle.

Wetherby allowed himself a grim smile. I wager I overset her plans this morning. She was off to warn Pym or I don't know her mind. Rather annoyed to see my man on the roof, wasn't she? Ha! I'd put him in her parlor if I could. He'd be more use than that stupid girl . . . Lisbet? Lily? Lilian! The corners of Lord Wetherby's mouth drew down in disgust.

If her ladyship stirs one foot beyond her gate, she'll be followed and arrested. I don't care if she's delivering victuals to the poor. And when she's in the Tower, the King will have no one to thank but me. He won't thank me though. He doesn't even see her treachery.

Such a little, little man, Wetherby thought. Still, he is the King.

Lord Wetherby sent two guards to circle the crowd. It was more a gesture than a necessity. He'd already posted guards close to the King's coach and sent many spies among the people.

She'll send messengers, he thought. She'll not give up easily. Lord Wetherby rehearsed the long list of Lady Carlisle's friends and family. At every name he shook his head. None of these people had seen her ladyship today. They wouldn't know of the threat to the traitors in Parliament.

The only coach to leave Lady Carlisle's mansion carried that brat of Baroness Wilthrop's and her maid. Lord Wetherby made a mental note to inquire into the loyalties of Lady Wilthrop. After all, any friend of Lady Carlisle's . . . My men sent the coach to St. James. If they were trying to deliver a message, they'll never get through.

Lord Wetherby jerked upright. Fool! He cursed himself. Two girls in the coach sent to St. James Palace. Two maids in the hallway who wouldn't answer when he addressed them. The two with Roland in the street . . . One had looked up for an instant—

Lord Wetherby turned in his saddle. "Guards!" he shouted. "To me. We are looking for two maids and a young courtier, Roland Stuart by name. Arrest them at all costs. They are traitors to the Crown." He spurred his horse, sending it lunging through the crowds around the King.

CHAPTER TWENTY-TWO

THE RIVER

"There!" a guard shouted. "Stop those three! The Commander wants them!"

Four guards, their swords drawn, charged their horses.

Roland turned to see who the guards were chasing. An arrest was always interesting. Perhaps a chase, some sword play, and the struggling captive begging for mercy.

It took all three of them several seconds to realize that the charging animals were headed straight for them. Roland whirled and pushed the girls toward the gate. "Go to the river bank and hide. I'll lead them away." He ran several steps and turned. "Run! Now!" Ellanor stood long enough to see him dodge the horses and sprint towards the deep shadows of St. James Park.

Ellanor and Priscilla fled through the gate and across the palace yard. Ellanor felt she couldn't run fast enough; she was tired, and the layers of clothes she wore caught at her knees and ankles. She stumbled forward, sure she would be caught. Priscilla ran by. She had lifted her skirts to free her feet.

"Where's a hiding place?" Priscilla ran along the river wall, first one way, then the other. "I thought Roland said we could hide here. There's nothing, not even any bushes."

"Perhaps he meant down by the river." Ellanor looked over the wall. The Thames was well below them. "It looks as if the current has just turned. Perhaps he meant down there."

"Mistress, we must hurry. The guards have come through the gate!"

Ellanor led Priscilla down slippery wooden stairs to a boat landing that shuddered against the pull of the strengthening current. The further they descended, the darker it became. The movement of the water reminded Ellanor of a huge, black snake.

One of the guards started down the steps. He shouted, "Stand, in the name of the King!"

"Under the steps! Quick!" Ellanor pulled Priscilla into a crouch. They heard the guard descending slowly, testing every step to keep from slipping.

"They down there?" another guard asked.

"They're down here, all right. And they're not going anywhere with the tide coming in and all," said the man on the stairs.

"Let's post a guard until morning when we can see what we're doing. I need a warm-up."

"Right! They'll be sorry they didn't surrender after they've spent a night down there!" The guard on the stairs shouted over his shoulder. "Hear that, young missies?" His harsh laughter echoed against the brick wall as he climbed to the top of the river bank.

For one wild moment Ellanor felt as though she and Priscilla were playing a game of All Hide.

"Now what?" asked Priscilla. "He's right; we'll either freeze to death or die of some disease carried on the night air."

Ellanor walked to the edge of the landing nearest the bank. "We can walk along the wall, but it's too far to jump. We'll have to wade."

"No, thank you very much. I'm wet enough and cold enough already." Priscilla sat under the stairs and wrapped her arms around her knees.

"Me, too, but we're trapped if we don't get off the landing. It's either stay here and be arrested in the morning or see if we can find a place to hide. There's still plenty of bank to walk on. It's our only way out." Ellanor sat down and put her feet in the river. The cold water took her breath away. The current pulled at her hems. She stretched one foot down to find how deep the water was. "It's only up to my knee. We can do this." Ellanor slid off the landing and into the river. The current nearly swept her feet from under her.

"Well, if I must." Priscilla eased her way into the water. She was shivering so much that Ellanor heard the chattering of her teeth and one word, "Cold!"

Leaning on each other for support, they waded to the muddy bank and collapsed against the rough stone wall. Priscilla drew back. "It's covered with slime!"

"Let's follow it a ways." Ellanor pressed her right hand against the wall's slippery surface and walked slowly along the bank. The gravel turned to ankle deep mud. At each step, the mud threatened to keep their shoes.

"Mistress, where are we going?"

Ellanor shook her head. "I don't know. I don't see any hiding places down here, do you?"

"I can't see anything." Priscilla pulled one of her feet free. The mud made a slow sucking noise. "This mud stinks," she said as an afterthought.

"How far have we come from the landing?" Ellanor asked.

Priscilla looked back over her shoulder. "I'll bet we've come far enough so that the old palace is above us."

"That means the next stairs should be inside the palace walls." Ellanor stared ahead. "Those torches ahead must mark them."

"I'll bet they're guarded. We'll have to find another way out of here." Priscilla took a step in front of Ellanor and stumbled into a hole carved by the current.

Someone shouted over the wall, "We know you're down there. There's no escape. Of course, you won't smell so good." The girls heard his laugh grow faint as he walked away from the wall.

Priscilla scrambled out of the hole. "I can hardly move, my clothes are so heavy with water."

"If he were going to follow us, he'd already be down here," said Ellanor.

"They don't have to follow us." said Priscilla. "All they have to do is wait until we come up or the current carries us away. We certainly can't use those stairs." She nodded toward the torches that marked the next stairway. Their bright flames were reflected in the rising river. "We must have missed Roland's hiding place."

Ellanor felt her own strength was nearly gone. "How could there be a place to hide down here? The tide will cover everything. We have to keep moving."

Priscilla walked slowly ahead bracing herself against the wall.

Ellanor heard a scream and the scrabble of pebbles. When she looked up, Priscilla had disappeared.

"Priscilla? Priscilla?" Ellanor stepped forward, and the wall disappeared under her hand. "Priscilla? Where are you?"

Priscilla ran into Ellanor and screamed again. Ellanor hugged her and held her tight. They stood like two joined statues.

Finally Priscilla said, "I fell sideways into this hole in the wall. We'd better get out of here before the river rises too high."

"Wait. Maybe this is one of the hiding places Roland meant. If it is a hiding place, it must be safe when the river is high. It's pitch black in here. I wish I could see . . ."

"Didn't Roland give you his candle and tinderbox?"

"Yes!" Ellanor patted her pocket. "Here's the candle . . . and the box. Here, hold the candle."

Priscilla patted Ellanor's shoulder and arm until she found the candle in her mistress's hand and took it.

"I hope I can do this. My fingers are so cold." Ellanor struck the flint and a spark flickered. "There's a spark. Ah, here's a sliver of fat wood. If I can get it lighted, we'll be able to see what's here."

"Do we really want to?" Priscilla's voice was shaking.

Ellanor wasn't so sure, but she struck the flint again, and on the fourth try, the fat wood sputtered into a small flame.

Priscilla held the candle out, and Ellanor lit the wick. They stared at the light, happy to have it. Priscilla moved the candle slowly around. They were in a man-made cave in the river wall. The ceiling was about ten feet high, but it would be under water when the tide was fully in. The walls and ceiling were covered in green slime, and there was a thin layer of mud covering the gravel under their feet.

Priscilla moved toward the back of the cave.

"Mistress!" Priscilla whispered as though she had seen a ghost. "Look at this." She held the candle further in front of her to light the bottom steps of a stairway. "Shall we go?"

Ellanor shivered. If they took the time to find out where the steps went, they might not be able to get out to the river bank again. They might be trapped and drowned. On the other hand, someone had built the steps. They led somewhere.

Priscilla made up her mistress's mind. "I'm going up." She stumbled on the bottom step, caught herself, and began climbing. Ellanor followed. The bricks, rotten from years of being under water, crumbled under their weight. They staggered up the stairs, clutching at the wall for balance.

At the fifteenth stair, the cave turned to the left and climbed to a clay path, hard packed and level.

"Hold up the candle, Priscilla. Look," Ellanor scuffed her toe in the powdery clay. "This doesn't look like it's ever been under water. And the walls are dry. We must be above high tide. At least we won't drown."

Priscilla touched Ellanor's arm. "Listen."

"I hear it." Ellanor tried to still her breathing so she could listen. "Voices."

"I wonder where we are?" Priscilla spoke in a whisper.

"We must be inside the old palace walls. Let's go on, but we'd better be quiet. If we can hear them, they'll be able to hear us." Ellanor motioned for Priscilla to proceed.

They walked on dust now. The voices gradually died away. Then the passage ended. It was closed with a wooden panel.

"Now what?" Priscilla's teeth chattered with cold.

Ellanor stepped past her maid. "Why would it just end? Surely there's an opening somewhere."

"Perhaps it's an old exit to the river that's been blocked up."

Ellanor ran her hands over the rough wood. Then she ran her fingers around the edge where the wood and the brick wall met. She heard a dry click and the panel swung inward. Warm air flowed into the cave.

Ellanor reached into the darkness beyond the door and felt the folds of heavy drapery. She knelt and lifted the lower edge. By light coming in through windows she could see the walls of a small room and a doorway in the opposite wall. The fireplace was cold, and there was no light showing under the other door. Ellanor crawled under the drapery and into the room.

She walked around and peered out the windows. When she reached the doorway again she said, "Blow out the candle, Priscilla, and come through."

Priscilla handed the candle to Ellanor. "Where are we?"

"Somewhere in the old palace." said Ellanor. She went to the door on the other side of the room and pulled the latch. The door swung open with a rusty screech.

Ellanor and Priscilla froze. There were no rushing footsteps, no shouting voices, just dull noises from people somewhere a long distance away.

Ellanor squeezed through the half-opened door; Priscilla followed. The next room was considerably larger. It held three beds with blankets and three chairs at a table. Over everything lay a thick layer of dust.

Priscilla sat on one of the beds and pulled the blanket around her. Ellanor sat on another bed and used its blanket to soak up some of the water in her cloak, skirts, and stockings. She tried to remove the mud on her shoes. "Clean up as best you can. We still have to find Mr. Pym."

"What?" Priscilla sat in a cloud of dust particles.

"I don't know how it happened, but we can't be far from Parliament. If we are inside the old palace, we're near St. Stephen's Chapel."

"It seems like hours have passed. Surely he's been arrested by now." Priscilla sneezed.

"Really, I don't think we were down by the river that long. Anyway, we can't just sit here. We might as well try to do what we set out to do." Ellanor put her hand in the ring pocket and felt its cold metal.

"All right, but we look a fright. We need more than a quick sopping up."

Ellanor stood up after cleaning her shoes. "If I wrap my cloak around me, is it too obvious that I've been wading in the Thames?"

Priscilla studied her. "It's hard to tell in this light."

"My shoes whish with every step."

"If we are in a darkened passage, no one will notice too much, except . . ." Priscilla wrinkled her nose.

"What?"

"That slimy river smell . . . We're not going to get rid of that."

"Perhaps we can pass as cleaning maids. No one expects much from them. At least we're dressed for the part. Tuck your hair back under your cap, and let's find our way out of here."

"I wonder where Roland is." said Priscilla.

"I hope he got away." Ellanor pulled her cap down around her face and wiped her muddy hands on the blanket. "That's it. Ready?"

"Ready." Priscilla followed her mistress into a dimly lighted passageway.

"Look for a door to the outside." Ellanor whispered over her shoulder.

They heard a faraway burst of laughter. A door opened ahead, allowing the glow of candlelight to flow down the passage. Then it closed, and all went back into shadow. They reached the door to the laughter and light. Ellanor opened it a crack.

"There are a lot of men in there. We have to go through. If we stay along the walls, in the shadows . . ."

CHAPTER TWENTY-THREE

WARNING

Priscilla looked at her mistress in the dim light. "Wait," she said. "You don't half look a sight. Now that we can see better, let me tidy you a bit." She tucked stray curls under Ellanor's cap and brushed dirt and cobwebs from the ruffle around her face. She pulled Ellanor's cloak straight before stepping back to inspect her work. "I can't do anything with your shoes. They're in an awful state."

"My feet feel like blocks of ice. Now, let me look you over." Ellanor set Priscilla's cap straight and wiped smudges of dirt from her face. She brushed Priscilla's cloak with her hand. "Perhaps our cloaks will hide our shoes well enough."

"Where will you find Mr. Pym?"

Ellanor rubbed her hands together to warm them. "In St. Stephen's Chapel. That's where Parliament meets. Someone will know where he is."

"And you'll walk right up to him? Looking like this?" Priscilla pointed at her muddy clothes.

"I don't know. I haven't thought that far. I hope he recognizes me, but we have to find him first. . . . Let's go." Ellanor took a deep breath, opened the door, and stepped into the room.

Dozens of candles burned, making Ellanor squint against the light. The warm air felt suffocating. She lowered her head and walked as close to the wall as possible. From the corner of her eye she saw dozens of men. Some huddled in small groups. Others walked in twos and threes. A few sat by themselves reading. A couple turned to look at two of the dirtiest cleaning wenches they'd ever seen.

"I wonder if they cleaned these chambers?" asked one.

"If so, the filth here must have been extraordinary!" came the answer. They chuckled and went back to their conversation.

Ellanor and Priscilla passed through a broad double door into a large outer chamber. It was cooler and not as brightly lit. A few small torches were set in sockets on the pillars. Benches lined the stone walls. Here men left their cloaks with their servants before moving into the room the girls had just left.

Ellanor led Priscilla along the wall, keeping the pillars between them and the men. They went down seven or eight steps and out into the cold night.

"No one stopped us!" Priscilla sounded as relieved as Ellanor felt.

Ellanor pointed at a figure watching coaches arrive. "Look. There's a servant. Let's ask him where the chapel is." She walked over and gave a quick curtsy. "Pardon me. I have a message for a minister of Parliament. I am to meet him outside St. Stephen's Chapel. Where is that?"

"Just behind you." He pointed to the building they had just left. "Didn't I see you coming out just now?"

"Yes, but I had no idea where I was. I've not been here before."

The servant wrinkled his nose and backed away from them.

"Please, I have an urgent message for a minister of Parliament, but my mistress sent me with instructions that are not perfect."

"You look as if you were caught in the rain a few minutes ago."

For the first time Ellanor noticed the paving stones were wet. "Oh, yes, . . . yes, we were."

"No one cares for us folk, eh?" he asked. "Send us out in weather like this. Keep us hanging about at their every whim. I'm about frozen to the bone waiting for my master, I am."

"Will you help me? I'm looking for Mr. Pym. You haven't seen him this evening, have you?" Ellanor looked around at the coaches still arriving in the courtyard.

"No. Haven't seen him. Maybe he's not arrived yet."

"Is there anyone I could ask—"

"There he is, right there." The servant swung his arm up and pointed. "Move quickly. He'll be hard to find once he's inside."

"Thanks ever so much." Ellanor said. She and Priscilla turned to follow Mr. Pym.

"There! Stop them! Those three, right there!" Lord Wetherby spurred his horse through the crowd. His sword glinted in the torch light.

The servant looked up. "Who? He means us. What for? What's—?"

Ellanor hesitated for half a breath then grabbed a handful of Priscilla's cloak and ran toward Mr. Pym. Lord Wetherby's horse shouldered his way between them, tearing Priscilla's cloak from her mistress's hand. Ellanor fell to her knees. When she looked up, she saw Priscilla scramble to her feet and run out of the courtyard with two of the King's Guard spurring their horses after her.

Ellanor pushed herself to her feet and started after her maid. Lord Wetherby had turned his horse and was riding straight at her. Ellanor turned back to the chapel, ran through the crowd of men into the outer chamber and up the stairs into the darkest corner she could find.

Guards forced their way through the door.

Tears of exhaustion and frustration ran down her face. Ellanor leaned against a pillar. I've lost Mr. Pym . . . failed Lady Carlisle. The guards will catch Priscilla and throw her in the Tower. But, we're not arrested yet, and neither is Mr. Pym, she told herself. She pushed away from the pillar. "I'll find Mr. Pym, one way or another," she said aloud.

"Did I hear my name? Who called?" A man stopped not more than four steps from Ellanor.

"Mr. Pym? Is it you, sir?" Ellanor gulped. "I have a message for you."

John Pym was dressed in sober black. His only ornament was a silver clasp that held his cloak around his shoulders. He looked her over, not recognizing his supper hostess of a few weeks before. "I don't give money to beggars."

Ellanor shook her head. "No, . . . no money. It's Lady Carlisle, she's sent—"

"Quietly, wench. Some names should not be spoken aloud tonight." He led Ellanor back to the dark behind the pillar. He sat on a bench and studied her appearance. "You are from her ladyship? How do I know?"

Ellanor pulled Lady Carlisle's ring from her pocket and held it up. "Sir, don't you recognize me?"

Mr. Pym took the ring. After he had studied it well, he said, "This is her ladyship's ring. Speak."

A commotion at the door distracted Ellanor. She looked out in time to see Lord Wetherby stride in. Where was Priscilla? Had she escaped?

"Girl? Time is pressing. The message!"

Ellanor whirled back around and bent close to Mr. Pym. "Her ladyship waited on the Queen this morning and learned that the King is coming here to arrest you and your friends. I have just arrived to warn you."

"You're certain? My friends as well?"

Ellanor nodded.

Mr. Pym stood up and motioned another man over to him. They spoke for a brief time, then Mr. Pym returned to Ellanor. "Wait here. My secretary will find the others and bring them here. Tell them I've gone to arrange our transportation."

"Yes." Ellanor sank down on the bench and leaned her head against the wall behind her. We've done it, she thought. We didn't fail, Priscilla. For a moment she'd forgotten Priscilla! Ellanor pushed herself to her feet. Mr. Pym had been warned. She had to find her maid.

Someone touched her shoulder.

Ellanor jumped and grabbed her skirts. She wasn't going to be caught now! Before she could take two paces, someone held her by the arm.

"Miss? Don't be alarmed. Mr. Pym's secretary sent us here. Where is he?"

Ellanor shook her head. "I don't know. He went to find a way for you to leave. You are to wait here for him."

"Ah, here he is," said one of the men.

Mr. Pym joined the group. "I've procured a boat. We have only to reach the river by the old postern gate. Come." The men moved away from the bench. Mr. Pym turned. "Miss? We're not leaving you behind. You're responsible for our being able to escape arrest at all."

Ellanor forced her tired legs to move. She heard a crash of weapons and shouts of His Majesty's Guardsmen, "Make way for His Majesty!"

Mr. Pym stopped short. "We can't leave this way. Holles, you know this chapel well. Is there another way? We have a boat at the landing if we can get there."

The man called Holles shook his head. "Gentlemen, I don't believe we can get out of here without a fight."

"I'm ready to fight," said the youngest man. "I'm innocent of any charges the King has against me."

"William, you're a fool. You may have to seal your innocence with your blood if you don't come away." His friends took hold of Mr. Strode's cloak and dragged him back into the shadows.

"I know a way out."

All six men turned toward the voice.

Ellanor stepped forward. "I know a way to the river. But your boatmen must pull along the wall until they are below this building. There is a cave cut in the river wall."

"You can get us to the river? Without going past the guards?" Mr. Pym asked.

Ellanor nodded.

"You're certain?"

Ellanor patted her damp clothes. "That's how I came in."

Mr. Pym hesitated only a moment. "We don't have much choice, gentlemen. Holles, where's that boy of yours?" He bent down and whispered instructions to a boy of about twelve. They watched him walk toward the door blocked by two guards. When he reached the door, he dived under the guard's outstretched arm. The last his master saw of him were his heels as he ran into the courtyard.

"John," said Mr. Pym, "walk with our messenger. She looks as if she might collapse at any moment." To his friends he said, "Gentlemen, we must follow quickly without drawing too much attention."

Ellanor led them into the chapel. Any order in the chapel was now gone. Chairs lay on their backs and sides. Writing tables had been knocked askew by men who rushed to see the disturbance.

Ellanor followed the muddy trail that she and Priscilla had left behind earlier. Like bread crumbs on a path, she thought. She heard the confusion of men reentering the chapel and furniture being set straight, but didn't look up. She stopped at the small doorway.

Someone whispered in her ear, "Are you sure?" She nodded.

"There! Stop those men," someone shouted. "In the name of King Charles, surrender!"

Ellanor slipped through the door; the men followed and slammed it behind them. She hurried down the dusty passage to the room with the beds where she and Priscilla had tried to tidy themselves. The men moved the beds against the door.

The King's guards thudded down the passage.

Ellanor entered the room that overlooked the river and pulled out her candle and tinderbox. Her fingers wouldn't work. It was Mr. Pym's secretary who lit the candle and held it high while she pulled the drapery back and pushed the wooden panel open.

Behind them heavy thumps, a loud crash, and shouting told them the door to the bed chamber had given way.

Ellanor led the men into the cave. The last man arranged the old velvet draperies and closed the panel. They followed her through the dust and cobwebs, over the damp clay, and finally down the crumbling stairs. The scuffling and shouting behind them faded as the surge and splash of the river grew louder.

She halted at the top of the stairs. In the faint light of the candle she saw that the river covered some of the steps. She had no idea how many. She put her hand against the slimy wall to steady herself and went down. With hardly a second thought, she stepped into the cold water. It came to just above her knees. She heard the men whistle through their teeth when they stepped into the water.

The swirls and eddies of the river's current caught her legs. She slipped and lost her footing. The secretary's arm went around her waist and held her upright. The cave had seemed much longer when she and Priscilla had first come through it.

"Is the boat there?" Holles asked. "Did my boy get through?"

The secretary waved the candle then dropped it in the water. The signal was answered by the dull rattle of oars in oarlocks. The bow of a boat appeared across the mouth of the tunnel. Ellanor felt herself lifted over the side. She slipped off the seat to the bottom of the boat. Under the back seat was Mr. Holles's boy.

"Hope you don't mind, guv'nor," said one of the oarsmen. "He didn't want to miss the excitement."

CHAPTER TWENTY-FOUR

Priscilla felt her cloak tear free. She was lifted from the ground and landed with a heavy thump on the pavement. She lay for a moment to recover her breath, then scrambled to her feet.

"Mistress? Mistress!" Priscilla couldn't see Ellanor anywhere.

Two guards turned their horses toward her. She pushed through a group of bystanders and fled from the courtyard. Her wet hems wrapped themselves around her legs and made it hard to run. She lifted her skirts, dashed across the road, and fled into the shadows of St. James Park.

Someone ran alongside her. Priscilla gave her last bit of energy trying to outrun the dark figure. A hand reached out and grabbed her shoulder. Priscilla slipped on the wet grass.

Her pursuer fell with her. A hoarse voice whispered in her ear. "Would you stop thrashing about?"

Priscilla ignored the warning and struck with both her fists. Her captor caught them both and held them fast in one hand. His free hand came down roughly on her mouth. In the short silence, Priscilla heard the guards pull their horses to a halt just inside the park. She stopped struggling.

The riders decided that their duty lay with keeping the peace around St. Stephen's Chapel rather than braving the gloom of the park. They turned their horses toward the lights of the street.

The man lifted Priscilla to her feet and led her further into the dark, but now he was limping badly. She stumbled along beside him, angry with him for dragging her away from her mistress. Priscilla dug her heels into the grass and jerked free. Her captor's exclamation of surprise and pain gave her the satisfaction of knowing that she'd caught him off guard.

She ran back toward the crowds and bobbing torches. Her feet felt like blocks of ice. Her breath came in rasping gasps. Behind her the uneven thud of heavy boots grew louder. She had almost reached the line of oak trees that marked the park boundary when an arm grabbed her around her waist. Her captor rolled with her back into the shadows. Priscilla's fists began their work on his head and shoulders.

"Stop!" he whispered between gasps. "It's me! Priscilla!"

She hesitated, both fists poised to strike. "Roland?"

"Shhh! Yes. What are you doing here?"

"I have to get back to the courtyard!"

Roland pushed Priscilla away and sat up. "What are you doing in the park?" he asked again.

"Running from the guards."

"I saw that, but why? Where's Ellanor?"

Priscilla shook her head. "I don't know. Lord Wetherby recognized us. I have to go back—"

"Wetherby! You can't. They'll arrest you."

"I must."

Roland pushed himself to his feet and balanced on his good leg. "Let's move into the shadows. Tell me what happened, and we can decide what to do."

Priscilla supported him as he hopped to a great oak tree. They sat down and leaned against the rough bark. Roland stretched his left leg out. "I twisted my knee when we fell back there."

"Sorry. I didn't know who you were."

"It's nothing. Now, tell me what has happened."

"We'd just found Mr. Pym when Lord Wetherby rode us down. I was thrown to one side, and when I got up, she was gone." Priscilla wagged her head back and forth and shivered. She felt like crying. "He might have killed us! I don't know if my mistress is alive or . . . or . . ."

Roland shifted closer to Priscilla and put his arm around her shoulders. He was shivering as much as she was. "If we sit closer, it might warm us up a bit," he said. "She's probably fine. You're not badly hurt, are you? Bruised a bit? Why should Ellanor have been injured any more?"

Priscilla took a deep breath through her chattering teeth. "I hope so. How did you get here?"

"I ran into the park after you headed for the river bank. Then I tried to get into St. Stephens without being recognized. I thought I could warn Mr. Pym if you and Ellanor weren't able to. I've been watching for you and Ellanor. I circled around, but I didn't see either of you."

"You'd never have found us. We were down by the river."

"Down *by* the river?

"We were looking for the place to hide you told us about."

"I didn't know of any particular place. I just hoped there would be some place you could hide. Is that how your clothes got so wet?"

Priscilla nodded. "We ran down to the landing. A guard stood at the top, so we waded to the bank and walked along the wall. I nearly went in face first when I stepped in a hole. Anyway, we found a tunnel. It was still dry so we went in."

"That was dangerous with the tide coming in. If you'd been caught in there, you'd have drowned."

"Actually, it was a good thing because there were stairs at the back that led to an old passageway. It must have been blocked off for years. Mistress found the latch to the door that let us into a room. The dust was inches thick. We could hear people talking so we walked towards that. We didn't know where we were and walked right through the Chapel. We were standing in the courtyard talking to a servant when Lord Wetherby crashed in." Priscilla shivered again and leaned closer to Roland.

He nodded. "I saw him charge you and saw you run into the park, but you didn't come close to me. I didn't see Ellanor. There was nothing for it but to follow you and try to keep you safe from the cutpurses."

"I must get back." Priscilla tried to get up and fell back with a moan. "My muscles have cramped."

Roland struggled to his feet and leaned against the tree. "You're right. We need to find Ellanor and warn Mr. Pym." He pulled Priscilla up beside him. "Mind if I use your shoulder?"

Priscilla couldn't feel her toes, and her legs felt as if she'd lost all control of them. She could barely hold herself up let alone Roland as he leaned more and more on her. They hadn't managed a dozen steps before he slipped to the ground and sat bent over pressing his hands against his knee.

"I can't do it," he said through clenched teeth.

Priscilla knelt beside him. "You wait here. I'll go see what's happening."

"Priscilla! No!"

Roland's hoarse whisper was too late. Priscilla was already moving toward the edge of the shadows. There were guards along the street and men shouting in the courtyard. His Majesty was leaving the chapel. Lord Wetherby was not to be seen. Neither was Ellanor. Nor was Mr. Pym.

A guard saw Priscilla and spurred his horse toward her. "Halt, in the name of the King!" He shouted. "Halt!"

Priscilla backed away from the torches, turned, and ran. After staring at the bright torch light, she couldn't see in the shadows. She stumbled over roots and fought her way through thickets. Her ears were full of thundering hooves and the shouting of the guard.

Suddenly, there was no sound of either galloping horse or shouting guard, only her own ragged breathing. She stopped and heard Roland's whisper, "To your left, your left!" Guided by his whispered directions, she found him in the shelter of a thicket.

"What happened? Where's the guard?" Her whisper seemed loud in the silence.

Roland put his finger to her lips.

They heard what sounded like a muffled cry not too far away, then nothing. Priscilla began to breathe again. "This be an uncomfortable place to spend the night," said a voice.

Roland and Priscilla became as still as statues.

"I think ye'd best come with us." To some other men he said, "Bring 'em along, gents."

Roland groaned when rough hands pulled him from under the thicket and set him on his feet.

"Stop!" Priscilla's command halted all activity. "Don't you see my friend is injured?"

At a nod from the leader, two of the men put their arms around Roland and half carried him along. Priscilla followed, resolving not to let him out of her sight.

They walked through the dark, barely able to see each other and the trees that surrounded them. Priscilla lost track of direction and then of time. Finally she saw the flicker of a fire through the trees. That's where they'll take us, she thought. We'll be beaten and robbed and left for dead. Then she nearly laughed out loud. Robbed? Of what?

The one who had spoken to them stopped to speak in low tones to a man who appeared out of the shadows.

In the camp the men placed Roland close to the fire. Priscilla held her hands out to the heat. The leader stood opposite them.

"Ned, they be a scraggly pair," said a man who sat just outside the circle of light. "Ye think to make your fortune from them, do ye?"

Several others laughed.

"No fortune from them, I think," Ned said. "They look poorer than they ought considering the crowd they were working." He smiled. "Even the King were there and other elegant dressers." He spoke to Roland, "Didn't ye lift anything a'tall?"

Lift? Priscilla looked at Roland. To her surprise he said, "The guards recognized us. Our pockets remain empty, much to our embarrassment. And I have twisted my knee running to escape."

Ned stepped closer to the fire. He was a short, thin man. His unkempt hair stood almost straight up over his face. When he spoke, there were gaps where teeth should have been. "Never let it be said Ned's hospitality is stingy."

Both of them were handed a wooden bowlful of stew and thick pieces of brown bread.

"Eat," said Ned. "We'll talk when ye've finished."

Priscilla didn't wait for a second invitation. The bowl of stew was hot and tasted better than any dish she could remember.

"There's little meat," said the cook. "We've had a run of ill luck that's put a proper stew beyond our pocket."

"Ill luck which these two have ended." Ned motioned two of his men forward. "Look what we found chasing 'em."

The men dropped a guard's uniform, a sword and short sword, two pistols with powder and shot, a belt, hat, boots, spurs, stockings, gauntlets, and shirt.

"Did you leave him with nothing?" Priscilla stared at the pile of clothes and weapons.

"Aye. He were marching back to his friends in his shift and drawers." The first robber spoke and the second nodded in agreement.

"His horse?" Roland asked.

"Aye, we have that and his saddle and bridle. As Ned says, ye brought us grand good luck, ye did."

Priscilla laughed with the men.

"Oh, and there be a purse. Not terrible heavy, but enough for our simple needs until we can sell the rest." Ned added the leather wallet to the pile. "Since ye brought these riches to us, so to speak, would ye be making a claim against any of it?"

Priscilla looked at Roland who shook his head. "We lay no claim. If we brought this to you, you've more than repaid us with fire and food," he said.

Grateful responses came from all around them.

Priscilla felt the heat from the fire working its way through the layers of her clothes. She could even feel her toes beginning to tingle. Her muscles relaxed. In spite of the strong smell of the river rising from her skirts and the taste of stew on her tongue, her eyes closed and she fell against Roland.

"Poor lass," said a short man with a striped scarf wrapped around his neck and head. "I saw the guard run her down. She took a terrible fall, she did; it's a wonder she's not hurt." He turned to Roland. "Where were ye when the guards came? I didn't see ye until the lass ran from the courtyard."

Roland decided to tell as much of the truth as he could without mentioning Mr. Pym. He nodded to Priscilla. "She and another came in through the side gate and I went in the main gate. With Parliament meeting and all, we thought there was good opportunity to shift somewhat from their pockets to ours."

"Oi, a treasure trove there for the taking," said the man with the scarf.

"Then the guards arrived." Roland hung his head. "We were recognized too quickly."

"So young and already ye have a reputation? Tha must be ver' good or ver' bad at the trade to be so well known." The man with the scarf peered at them.

Roland smiled. "I think we're quite bad at it, really."

"Nah, the idiot on the great horse charged." The man with the scarf spit into the fire. "Ye had no chance."

"We were fortunate to escape." Roland shuddered. They had been fortunate.

"And the third one?" asked Ned.

"In the tumult, we lost sight of our friend."

"I hope he's safe and sound as ye are." Ned paused. "That commotion wasn't all over the likes of ye, was it?"

"It seems that someone of great importance was to be arrested," Roland said.

"Must have been mighty important to bring the King hisself out. But, I see you're as tired as the girl." Ned motioned toward Priscilla. "Let Harry tend to your leg. He has a fine way with curing animals. He'll do well by ye. Sleep now."

"We thank you for your kindness. We should be on our way—"

"Nah. You're protected here. We'll wake ye before the sun rises and set ye in whichever direction ye like." Ned grinned. "We have to be gone as well. But, for now, take your ease." To one of his men he said, "Bring those blankets here."

The men settled Priscilla in several layers of blankets, close to the fire. After Harry declared nothing broken and bound his knee, Roland rolled up in the rest of the blankets and fell asleep the moment his eyes closed.

CHAPTER TWENTY-FIVE
RESCUE

The oarsmen pushed out to the middle of the river. The boat
and its cargo disappeared against the dark water. The tide ran full
against them.

Mr. Pym asked, "You know where to go?"

"Aye, guv'nor," came the low answer, "to London. I'm thinking
we'll set you down at Blackfriars."

Mr. Pym nodded to the dark shadow of the boat master.

Ellanor listened for the sound of horses' hooves and men shouting
along the riverbank. She heard only the river slapping at the boat.
Someone pulled her close to try to warm her.

Where were Priscilla and Roland? Her fingers still felt the cloth
of Priscilla's cloak being pulled from her fingers when the horse ran
between them. What if she lay injured in the courtyard with no one
to help her? Was she hiding somewhere shivering in the cold? What
if she had been arrested? Ellanor felt hot tears roll down her cheeks.
She must tell Mr. Pym about Priscilla.

The lights of Westminster disappeared behind a bend in the river,
and the walls of the City appeared. The oarsmen pulled toward the
north shore and tied the boat fast to Blackfriars landing.

The man named John steadied Ellanor as she climbed out of the boat, and he helped her climb the stairs from the river. When she looked back, the boat was gone.

"Mr. Pym?" Ellanor reached out and touched the man's sleeve.

Mr. Pym turned immediately. "Yes?" He peered closely at Ellanor. "We all need some warmth, you especially." He led them to a small inn.

The innkeeper took one look at their wet and muddy clothes and put up his hand to refuse them entrance, but when he heard the jingle of Mr. Pym's purse, he bowed low before its coins. With a flourish he ushered them into his best parlor and built up the fire. To his delight, Mr. Pym commanded a large supper. Mr. Holles's boy went to the kitchen to eat.

Mr. Pym led Ellanor to the settle inside the fireplace. "Now, young miss," he began, "let us thank you properly." He reached up and pushed back her cap. "I say! Mistress Fitzhugh? You? You saved us? Why didn't you say something when you gave me the ring?"

The secretary whirled around. "Ellanor?"

Ellanor looked up into the face of Lord Netherfield.

"How in the world . . . ?" he began.

Mr. Pym took one of Ellanor's hands between his own. "That is exactly my question. If you have strength enough to tell us, that is."

Ellanor dragged her cap off her head. Her hair came down in tangled curls. "Priscilla." She said to Mr. Pym. "She's my maid. I don't know what's become of her. She was knocked to the ground by Lord Wetherby's horse, and when I looked for her, she was gone."

Mr. Pym gave one of his friends quick instructions. "She must be found quickly!" he said. "If she's been arrested, she must be freed by any means possible. That maid can be connected both with this young lady and with Lady Carlisle." To Ellanor he said, "We'll begin the search immediately. Mr. Hampden will see to it. You have my word on this."

"Thank you!" Ellanor wiped away her tears. "I'm sorry. I'm so afraid for her. And, Roland. He was there too. I don't know about him either."

Mr. Pym patted her hand and sat down beside her. "There's nothing to be sorry for. Most likely, you've saved our lives. We'll do all we can to help. We'll look for them both."

"A messenger should be sent to Lady Carlisle," said Mr. Holles. He stepped away from the fireplace speaking under his breath. "If that woman sent this poor child on such an errand, well . . ."

Mr. Pym said, "Let's hear the story first, Denzil." He turned back to Ellanor.

Most of the men now stood close by the fire. The room smelled of drying wool and dirty river water.

Ellanor wiped her face with her hands and cleared her throat. "Lady Carlisle arrived home early this afternoon . . ." Ellanor paused. "She waited on the Queen, who told her that the King intended to arrest you in Parliament this evening."

"Doesn't that sound just like His Majesty?" Mr. Holles asked no one in particular. "Has to have his own way and make a show of it."

"What about that lout, what's his name . . . Wetherby? I see his hand in this. I don't believe the King would have done it without some strong urging." Mr. Burton spoke while he was taking off his shoes. "Look at my stockings, will you? How shall I explain this to Mrs. Burton?"

"Hopefully she'll be happy that you're still alive." Mr. Pym spoke over his shoulder.

Mr. Burton sat down and propped his bare feet in front of the fire.

"Do go on, Ellanor," said Mr. Pym.

"Lady Carlisle was beside herself, knowing she couldn't get a message to you, sir. You know, she's been watched by Lord Wetherby's men. One was on the roof overlooking her garden! . . . I thought Priscilla and I might get through. After all you had invited me to hear a debate. I could send you a note from the gallery. It seemed so simple."

The maids laid the table and pulled benches and chairs around. The ringing of a bell announced the arrival of the soup. Without a word, everyone moved to the table. Mr. Pym took a seat at Ellanor's right. Lord Netherfield sat at her left.

Sir Arthur Heselrig stood. "Gentlemen, as one of those rescued today by the bravery of this young woman, I deem it absolutely necessary that we not only thank our great God for this meal, but that we also give thanks for His mercies in sending us our own guiding angel. Let us also request his especial mercy for her friends." All bowed their heads while he prayed after the manner of the Puritans.

After the "Amen," all that could be heard for several minutes was the clink of spoons on bowls and the hearty supping of spoonfuls of soup. Ellanor was sure no soup had ever warmed her so well.

While they waited for the next course, Mr. Pym encouraged Ellanor to continue her story. She told them of being detoured to St. James and their decision to walk to Westminster dressed as maids. She told them of Roland—

"Oh, him! I know the lad," Mr. Bulstrode interrupted. "From the good side of the Stuart family."

"Roland knew who we were right away." Ellanor said. "He wouldn't be left behind. It was a good thing he came, or we would have never found our way so quickly to Westminster. It was Roland who told us to hide down by the river. We found the tunnel quite by accident."

"I'm amazed that you had the courage to go down to the river at this hour," said Mr. Pym. "The current is dangerous enough, and who knows what sorts of derelicts might have been down there."

"So we found the passageway and walked right through the Chapel without even knowing it was Parliament. It was in the courtyard that Priscilla was separated from me. Then I found you." Ellanor could feel her throat tightening. "Now I don't know where she is, or Roland either."

"Don't you worry. We've sent messages and runners to look for Priscilla. We shall do the same for Roland, though he sounds as if he can look after himself." Mr. Pym turned when the dining room door opened and the host of the public house carried in platters of fish and lamb.

Lord Netherfield spoke quietly. "I never guessed it was you, Mistress Ellanor. Until we reached the inn, I had no inkling. You have more courage than most men I know. So does Priscilla. Please, don't worry about her. The search has already begun."

"Thank you." Ellanor swallowed more tears and wiped her eyes on her serviette. "I didn't know it was you either. I never expected to see you in Parliament."

"I'm Mr. Pym's secretary. You saved my life too. Thank *you*."

After dessert, the men took out their pipes and moved their chairs near the fire. Someone asked Mr. Burton if his socks were dry.

"Oh, yes, quite. But I'm afraid my shoes have gone stiff. I shouldn't have left them so close to the fire."

Lord Netherfield led Ellanor back to the settle beside the fire.

"My lord?" she asked, "Are you safe in London?"

He nodded. "Yes. The City will protect us. Many of the citizens here are no happier with His Majesty than we are."

"Shall I have to stay as well?"

"I've thought about that. It would be best if your absence from Lady Carlisle could be explained by a visit to my Aunt Esancy, . . . if that suits? Her house is in the City."

"I wouldn't like to greet her looking like this." Ellanor's fingers plucked her mud-stained woolen shift.

Lord Netherfield chuckled. "She'll love to make over you." He stood. "Gentlemen, I must see Mistress Ellanor to a safe house and dry clothing. I shall return in about an hour."

The innkeeper smiled and ordered a coach for Lord Netherfield and the dirty young woman. Many coins would find their way to his purse tonight.

CHAPTER TWENTY-SIX
HOMECOMING

"She's where?" Lady Wilthrop's eyebrows flew up and almost joined the curls on her head.

"She's with Lady Esancy for a day or two. I received a messenger from Lord Netherfield late last night to that effect." Lady Carlisle walked back and forth in Lady Wilthrop's sitting room. Her fan fluttered wildly.

"Why is she there? Why had I no notice of this? What has Lord Netherfield to do with anything?"

Lady Carlisle stopped in front of her friend and spread her hands like a criminal begging for mercy. "Forgive me. I'm so sorry. I never meant for her to become involved."

"Involved? With what?" Lady Wilthrop narrowly eyed her guest.

"This is all I know." Lady Carlisle threw out her arms and let them fall to her sides. "Some time ago Mr. Pym invited Ellanor to Commons to hear him speak. He was to deliver a speech yesterday evening, and I saw no harm. I myself have attended many times." Lady Carlisle hesitated. "I had to let her go, didn't I? There was no other way!"

Lady Wilthrop rose slowly from her chair. She was at least three inches shorter than Lady Carlisle, but her rigid posture made up for the lack. "No other way? Lucy?"

Lady Carlisle stepped back. "Well, . . . for Ellanor to hear Mr. Pym speak. Her maid accompanied her . . . and I sent my best driver. He was to escort her into and out of St. Stephens."

"Ellanor attended Parliament yesterday evening."

Lady Carlisle nodded. "Yes."

"During that absurd business when the King tried to arrest some of the members?"

"You've heard?"

"Everybody knows!" Lady Wilthrop's gesture included all of London and Westminster as well as a few suburbs. "My servants speak of nothing else. . . ." She returned to her chair. "Were you in any way involved?"

"Mary! How can you ask such a question?"

"How? As dear a friend as you are, Lucy, it's difficult to dismiss the constant rumors of your involvement at Court."

Lady Carlisle drew herself up. "Of course, I'm involved at Court. I am the Queen's confidant, you know."

"I do know. That's why I'm asking, was Ellanor in any way associated with the uproar at Parliament yesterday evening? And do sit down. Your wandering makes me dizzy."

Lady Carlisle sat down on a couch. "I wasn't there. How could I be involved? I did ask Ellanor to send a note to John on the floor of the Commons. Just a note of greeting, nothing more." The Countess clasped her hands in front of her. "Mary, you've ignored the rumors and slanders that caused others to turn their shoulders to me. I value your friendship far too much to presume upon it or to put Ellanor in jeopardy. Anyway, it's likely that neither the King nor Lord Wetherby even saw Ellanor."

"Lord Wetherby? He was there?"

Lady Carlisle snapped her fan shut. "If the King so much as takes three steps in the royal bedchamber, Wetherby is there. But even if he saw Ellanor, I doubt he recognized her. After all there were a number of people there. . . . Lady Esancy said that she hardly recognized the poor girl, exhausted, wet, mud—"

"Ellanor was what?"

"It . . . it rained, didn't it?" Lady Carlisle's voice went up in register. "It always rains here." She rushed into the explanation she'd rehearsed for an hour that morning. "The confusion of His Majesty's arrival kept Ellanor from reaching her coach. Lord Netherfield saw her and, at the time, it seemed best to him to take her to Lady Esancy's by river, and I agreed. They were on the river. It rained. They got wet."

"Why not take her to your mansion?"

"Have you ever tried to leave Parliament when everyone is calling for his coach?"

"She was with Lord Netherfield, at night, unchaperoned?"

"There's no cause for worry. Lord Netherfield is the soul of discretion. He'll say nothing."

"That's hardly the point, is it? This could ruin her marriage prospects."

"I also dropped a hint to the most reliable gossip I know that Ellanor has been visiting a dear elderly friend in the City since yesterday midday." Lady Carlisle made a mental note to speak with Lady Somerset as soon as possible.

"How I'll explain this lapse to her parents, I don't know." Lady Wilthrop took a deep breath and let it out slowly. "Perhaps the less said, the better. For now, anyway. Ellanor and Priscilla are safe."

"Ummm, not completely. Somehow the girls were separated. Both Lord Netherfield and Mr. Pym sent messages assuring me that everything is being done to locate Priscilla."

"Lucy, over twelve hours gone, and she's not found?"

"I truly don't know how this happened. If I'd only foreseen . . . but I couldn't have, could I?"

"Surely some word of Priscilla will come soon. I'll have some coffee and biscuits sent to us. I need something to clear my head." Lady Wilthrop gave instructions to a maid who hurried off.

By midmorning both women were pacing the floor. The coffee had grown cold. Neither any longer tried to make conversation. Lady Carlisle had torn her lace handkerchief to shreds, leaving bits of thread scattered about the room. Lady Wilthrop composed in her mind a letter to Priscilla's parents expressing her most sincere regrets.

The clatter of hooves and crunch of gravel outside sent both women rushing to the window. A coach skidded through the gate and careened around the corner of the mansion into the coach yard behind. The women gathered their skirts and ran to the yard entrance. Servants and maids scattered before them.

Three figures tumbled from the coach and scrambled toward the cellar entry.

"Get the horses and coach out of sight," shouted one of them. "And have one of the boys rake the gravel smooth. There must be no evidence that we've come here." With that he grabbed the other two, one by the arm and the other around the waist, and half-pulled, half-carried them into the cellars of the mansion.

Within moments, the horses were unhitched and stabled. The coach was wheeled into the coach house and wiped down. The gardener's boy finished smoothing the gravel just as five horsemen rode through the gate. The ladies ran back to the parlor.

"Wetherby!" Lady Carlisle gasped. "What's he doing—?" The pounding on the front door didn't let her finish.

"Sit down, Lucy." Lady Wilthrop handed her guest a cup half full of cold coffee. "I think we must act carefully."

"All those threads!" Lady Carlisle set her cup aside and went to her hands and knees picking up all the bits of her handkerchief she could reach. She slipped them under the edge of a carpet and retook her seat. When Fines bowed Lord Wetherby into the room, she was delicately sipping cold coffee.

Lady Wilthrop set her cup down and rose to meet her guest. "Ah, Lord Wetherby, what a compliment you pay me by calling."

Lord Wetherby bowed over her hand then gave a curt bow toward Lady Carlisle. "I'll not keep you long. I've come to collect the occupants of the coach that arrived here only moments ago."

"I beg your pardon? Coach? Whatever are you speaking of? None has come all day, except Lady Carlisle's, of course."

Lord Wetherby pushed past Lady Wilthrop and entered the next room.

"Why, yes, of course," she said, "feel free to stalk through my home without so much as a by your leave."

Lady Carlisle poured herself more cold coffee. "I see, Lord Wetherby, your manners are at their usual questionable standard."

The Commander of the Guard ignored both women and went to the front door. He waved the guards around to the back. "Search everywhere. Don't overlook a thing. We are looking for traitors against His Majesty!"

"Traitors? . . . Traitors!" Lady Wilthrop faced her visitor. "I remind you whose home you have entered!"

"Madam, you had best guard your tongue. I know very well whose house I have entered. There are traitors about; their coach turned in here. And your guest is not above suspicion." Lord Wetherby gave the Countess a mock bow. "Perhaps I shall have to post guards at your gate as I have at Lady Carlisle's?"

Lady Carlisle came to her feet at once. "Really, sir. You are too bold. Don't forget to whom you speak."

Lady Wilthrop saw Fines in the hallway out of Lord Wetherby's sight. He touched the side of his nose with his finger, gave a little nod, and backed away.

Lady Wilthrop relaxed. Fines's signal told her that whatever was going on, Lord Wetherby and his men would find nothing.

She returned to her chair and sat down. "You may post guards if you wish. If there are traitors here, my lord, I shall feel that much more secure. May I know the particulars of their crime? I feel somewhat entitled since you have entered my home." She heard banging doors and servants' protests at the back of the mansion as the guards searched the kitchen and storerooms.

Lord Wetherby swung around. "Perhaps you've heard about the riot at Parliament last night?"

Both women raised their eyebrows in question.

"Riot? Certainly not a riot, my lord." said Lady Carlisle. She set her cup and saucer on a small table.

"No? Well, it appears that chit of a girl you brought to London, Baroness, was at the heart of it. She prevented His Majesty from making an arrest!"

"Ellanor? My goodness! Why would Ellanor be anywhere near Parliament last night, or any night?" Lady Wilthrop asked. "She's been the house guest of a friend since yesterday afternoon."

"She was seen. . . . *I* saw her." Lord Wetherby's voice carried the sneer he was trying to keep from his face. "May I ask who this friend might be? We may wish to question her."

Lady Carlisle smiled. "You'd better be on your best behavior when you approach Lady Esancy."

"She was at St. Stephen's Chapel with her maid and that young Stuart fellow to warn Pym!"

Lady Carlisle tapped her fan against the palm of her left hand. "Lord Wetherby, if you, for a moment, believe that I would allow a young woman in my charge to go off unchaperoned for a second, you are—" She shook her head and turned away from him. "Words fail me. I truly don't know what you are."

"I know what *you* are. You drew that girl into your treachery. And when you couldn't get to Parliament yourself," Lord Wetherby smiled, "you sent her with a message to warn Pym of his arrest."

"Arrest! He can't be arrested while Commons is seated."

"If the King signs a warrant he can."

Lady Carlisle looked back over her shoulder. "Are we to assume that the attempt was successful?"

"You know it wasn't."

"I know nothing of this." Lady Carlisle raised her chin and turned to look directly at Lord Wetherby. "I do, however, feel much relieved hearing from so reliable a source that Mr. Pym was not arrested."

A guard entered the room. "We've found nothing, my lord."

"I saw the coach turn in here."

"Perhaps it went to another gate. We were some distance away."

Lady Wilthrop brushed a bit of lace around her wrist back into place. "An apology would now be acceptable . . . Commander."

Lord Wetherby turned on his heel and left the parlor.

Fines held the door wide for him.

CHAPTER TWENTY-SEVEN

FRIENDS

Fines closed the door behind Lord Wetherby and returned to the parlor.

Lady Wilthrop waited until Lord Wetherby's troops rode into the street before she turned to Fines. "Now," she said, "what's all this about?"

Before Fines could answer, Lord Netherfield peered around a corner. "They've left? Good. My lady, you must have a hundred questions. I will answer them all to your fullest satisfaction, I promise, but I must get these two to the City immediately. Only there will they be safe."

"Who must you take to London?" Lady Wilthrop looked from Lord Netherfield to Fines and back to Lord Netherfield.

"I have Priscilla and Roland, my lady." Lord Netherfield bowed.

"Well, I never! You have Priscilla? I've been frantic! She is unharmed? . . . Who's Roland?"

"They're both in the cellar."

Lady Wilthrop and Lady Carlisle pushed past Lord Netherfield and dashed through the passage leading to the cellar. At the bottom of the stairs stood the dirtiest girl either of them had ever seen.

"Oh my! Priscilla? Is that you?" Lady Wilthrop started down the stairs.

"Yes, Lady Wilthrop." Priscilla curtsied. "You'd best not come near me. I'm dirty, and I smell horrible."

Lady Wilthrop stopped. "My dear girl! Where have you been? What . . . ? Oh, dear me." She pulled her handkerchief from a pocket and held it over her nose. "You're quite all right?"

"Yes, just tired and dirty."

"Madam?" Fines held out his hand to help Lady Wilthrop back up the stairs. "Lord Netherfield wishes to speak with you about his plan for taking Priscilla and her friend into London."

Lord Netherfield had seated himself on the couch in the sitting room. He had run his fingers through his hair and straightened his rumpled clothing. His eyes were red-rimmed from lack of sleep. He held a half empty coffee cup. "Cold" was all he said.

Fines took a tray from a maid. It held a plate of fried sausages, tomatoes, eggs, bread, and mushrooms and a pot of fresh, hot coffee and buns. Fines set the tray on a small table and handed Lord Netherfield a fresh cup of coffee. "Careful, my lord, it's very—"

Lord Netherfield took a long swallow. He opened his mouth and breathed quickly in and out. "Hot!" He breathed in quickly to cool his tongue.

Fines pulled the table closer so his lordship could eat. When the plate was empty, Lord Netherfield turned to Lady Wilthrop. "Thank you!"

"My lord—" she began.

"I beg your pardon," he said, "but we haven't much time. The guards may return, and Priscilla, Roland, and I must be gone."

"Of course." Lady Wilthrop perched on the edge of her chair. "Where will you go? How?"

Lord Netherfield took another long drink of coffee. "I have a plan of sorts. First, may I have Fines for an hour or two?"

Lady Wilthrop nodded.

"Good. I also need to draw the guards Wetherby's posted away from here—"

"He's posted guards at my door? The nerve!"

"Indeed," said his lordship. "Look out the window. As I was saying, we need time to reach Ludgate. If you and Lady Carlisle will leave in your coach, I'm certain they'll follow you."

"That's your plan? To escape through the busiest gate in the City?" Lady Carlisle nearly shouted.

"It should make success all the more likely. Who'd be foolish enough to run from the guards on the main thoroughfares?" Lord Netherfield grinned and then became serious. "I'm hoping all the crowds in the streets will help hide us. We must leave immediately."

Lady Wilthrop nodded to Fines to have her coach brought around. "Do you want us to go anywhere special?"

"West, towards St. James. Keep them following you as long as you can. By the time they lose interest, hopefully, we'll be safe in the City."

Lady Wilthrop ran to the foot of the stairs. In a voice ladies almost never used, she shouted, "Martha! My cloak! And bring Lady Carlisle's maid! We're going on a very important outing!"

Lady Carlisle slipped her cloak over her shoulders. "We're going to be a diversion! How exciting!"

Lady Wilthrop's coach left in fewer than ten minutes. When three horsemen fell in behind them, Lady Carlisle commented that she had never been so happy to be followed by Lord Wetherby's lackeys.

Barely two minutes later, a cart full of bags and empty baskets joined other wagons and carts traveling to the City markets.

The old carter slouched on the rough wooden seat. He held the reins low between his knees as he guided his pony through the streets. His helper lounged beside him watching the street from under the brim of his hat. "Busy today," the younger man said.

"Right enough. You might get away with this."

The helper leaned back. "I don't see anyone paying us any attention," he said to a large basket and a pile of empty sacks. The cart rumbled and thumped down the Strand and into Fleet Street. The pony labored up the hill toward Ludgate.

"Guards at the gate!" The carter leaned toward his helper. "Worse luck, it looks like they're checking everything entering the City."

A shout came from a horseman wearing the uniform of the King's Guard. "Oi! Stop! Stop, I say!"

"Keep going," said the carter's helper. He leaned back to rearrange some lose bags. "Get ready to run."

A muffled voice said, "We're ready."

"Oi! You, in the cart!" The guard spurred his horse through the busy street.

"Keep going."

"We'll not make it to the gate," said the carter.

The guard was only a few feet away.

The helper leaned back. He grabbed the basket and heavy sacks and threw them to the street. "Run for the gate!"

Two figures struggled up from the bottom of the cart and flung themselves over the side. "This way," said Roland. He grabbed Priscilla's shoulder and limped alongside her.

The carter pulled his pony to a stop between the guard and Ludgate.

"Stop those two!" The guard shouted to two companions and pointed to two figures pushing through the gate. One of the guards cupped a hand to his ear and shook his head.

"You've blocked the street you stupid oaf," someone shouted.

"Don't blame me!" the carter answered. He jerked his thumb towards the guard. "He's the one who says I must stop in the middle of the street."

The carter's helper jumped down to lead the pony to one side, but made the tangle of animals and wagons worse. Carts crashed into each other. Horses reared, oxen bellowed.

The carter climbed down and took the pony's head. "Go, now, my lord," he said to his helper. "You can do nothing more here." His helper disappeared into the crowds.

The carter soothed his pony and gradually set both the pony and the cart to rights. He touched his cap to all who passed saying over and over, "Sorry guv'nor, sorry. Not my fault, you know."

The guard had to shout to be heard. "Where are they, old man? Tell me!"

The carter touched his cap to the guard and wagged his head from side to side. "Sorry, your worship. But Sophie here don't like the crowds. Sweet lass she is, but skittish. Nearly upset the cart, but we put it right, didn't we, girl?" He patted the pony's neck.

"I'm not your worship! Where are the two who jumped out of the cart?"

"Two? Nah, just my lad. Useless, he is. Run off to enjoy the pleasures of London, he has. He'll get the sharp edge of my tongue when next I see him. Be sure, your highness, he'll be properly spoken to." The carter touched his cap again.

The crowd flowed between the cart and the guard. Fines climbed onto the cart and touched his cap one last time to everyone in general. He called "walk on" to Sophie and headed back the way he had come. The guard could do nothing but sit his horse while the life of Fleet Street swirled around him.

Inside Ludgate, two vagabonds leaned against the warm stone wall. They also leaned against each other as though they were too weary to stand alone.

The carter's lad ran through the gate.

"Over here." The young man against the wall called out.

"All right there, Roland?" asked Lord Netherfield.

Roland reached down and rubbed his knee. "I can't go much farther."

"We'll take it as easy as we can, but we must move away from the gate."

"The guards can't arrest us in the City, can they?" Roland asked.

"Not legally, but they could catch us and drag us outside the City gates. Then they could arrest us."

"What put that guard on to us?" asked Priscilla.

"He was posted at the gate to check everyone who passed. It seems that Lord Wetherby wants to have a word with you two. Come." Lord Netherfield stepped beside Roland to support him. They joined the crowds milling around St. Paul's Cathedral and in Cheapside. He led them into narrow Bow Lane and from there through twisting alleys until he reached a heavy wooden door set in a high brick wall. When he pulled the cord, a bell rang deep inside.

Footsteps tapped across the stones. The porter peered through a small peep hole. Immediately he swung the gate open. A maid ran to tell her ladyship that her favorite grandnephew had arrived with two more guests.

Late that afternoon Priscilla awoke. The soft feather bed and pillow wrapped her in a warm cocoon. She wanted never to move again.

"Priscilla? Are you all right? Where have you been? What happened after the horse charged?" Ellanor couldn't get her questions out quickly enough.

"Mistress!" Priscilla sat up and groaned with the effort. "I'm stiff and sore all over. I shall have bruises for weeks." She leaned back on the pillows Ellanor placed behind her. "It's good to see you. Lord Netherfield said you delivered the message."

"We did it. We did it together. Mr. Pym and his friends are safe in London. I've been so worried for you."

"Where are we?"

"At Lady Esancy's. We came yesterday afternoon to visit for a few days."

"We did?"

Ellanor laughed. "Yes, we did."

"We're trying to keep the gossips at bay?" Priscilla pulled her down-filled coverlet straight.

Ellanor nodded. "Our reputations are secure."

"What happened to you, Mistress? All Lord Netherfield told us was that he saw you to safety before he came to find us."

"All will be told as soon as you are able to dress. Lady Esancy is on pins and needles to hear our adventures. And so are Lady Wilthrop and Lord Netherfield."

"They're here?"

"They have been waiting all afternoon for you and Roland to wake up. They declare they'll not leave until they've heard everything. When you're ready, I'll help you dress. Then we can go downstairs and have something to eat."

"If there's food, I'm ready now. I'm starving."

That evening Ellanor sat in front of the parlor fireplace, a heavy shawl around her shoulders. Lord Netherfield sat beside her reading from a broadside. "Parliament declares the King's proceedings against John Pym and his friends illegal, including all capital cases as treason and such like. The persons and goods of the members of both Houses are free from seizure until the Houses are convinced of their crimes and deliver them to the law. Any who try to arrest a Minister of Commons are publicly declared an enemy of that House." He laid the paper on a table. "How's that for a night's work, Mistress Ellanor?"

"Did you ever think working with Mr. Pym would be so dangerous?"

"Never. But it has been worth it. This morning, Parliament met the King in Guildhall. The Lord Mayor and Aldermen of London were there. His Majesty demanded the five men be turned over to him for what he calls a 'legal trial' for treason. However, he is no longer trusted, and the Lord Mayor refused. When His Majesty left Guildhall, people in the street shouted 'Privilege! Privileges of Parliament!' as he passed."

"All this because of a rumor about the Queen and the Irish Catholics." Ellanor stared into the fire. "Politics can be a dreadful business."

"Yes, but that same business can also protect us from the likes of Charles and Wetherby."

Ellanor smiled. "It was not politics that saved you from the Tower, my lord."

"True. Aunt Esancy says I should be on one knee kissing your shoe in thanks for my freedom."

Ellanor poked the toe of her shoe out from under her hems.

VISITORS

Two weeks later the King and Queen left Westminster for Hampton Court. Mr. Pym and his friends, accompanied by a grand procession of boats, returned up the Thames to Parliament. In February, Queen Henrietta Maria left for Holland while King Charles, the Prince of Wales, and Lord Wetherby rode north to York. Noble families left for their country estates unsure what either Parliament or the King would do next. It was rumored that Lady Carlisle had fled to the country.

A bone-numbing cold slowed all life. Winds from the North Sea blew icy rains across the country. Portions of the Thames froze. Every day came reports of people falling through the ice. Derelicts died in the street where they slept. The poor begged for lumps of coal and food. Lady Wilthrop contributed money, food, and blankets to her parish church, St. Clement Danes.

Ellanor and Priscilla returned to Lady Wilthrop's home after a week with Lady Esancy. Ellanor's lessons began again. A singing master came every Monday and Thursday at three o'clock. Lady Wilthrop herself taught Ellanor to play the lute. At least once each week, weather permitting, Ellanor attended a lecture on geography or natural history. Every Thursday afternoon she went over accounts with Lady Wilthrop. Ellanor found the mysteries of running a household as complex as those of history or French.

All the while Lady Wilthrop waited for an answer to a letter she'd written in mid-January. The spring thaw didn't hurry the mail, however. The ice melted and the rains continued making quagmires of the roads. It wasn't until late March that two letters arrived from Bishop's Manor. The first thanked Lady Wilthrop profusely for her care of Ellanor during the late tumults in London. Lady Wilthrop had neglected to mention Ellanor's part in those tumults. The second letter announced that the Fitzhughs would visit as soon as the roads were passable, perhaps in April.

Lady Wilthrop came up out of her chair much more rapidly than any lady of good breeding should have. April was only eight days away. Of course, they might come late in April, she thought, depending on the roads. Or they might appear at the door in eight days. Lady Wilthrop turned her household upside down in preparation.

Ellanor and Priscilla joined the commotion, grateful for the change of schedule. The tutors still arrived, and Ellanor met them faithfully, but she often took her lessons to the accompaniment of pounding hammers and the smell of wet plaster and paint.

"How can there be so much to do?" Ellanor asked Fines one day.

"Oh, Madam saves her little projects for just such a time as this. This way they all are done at once. Quite efficient, really."

Ellanor picked up a length of deep gold brocade. "What do you think of this for the curtains in the music room?"

Fines shook his head and walked away. "Oh, no. I'm not getting involved in those decisions."

At the end of eight days the house was ready, though the smell of paint was still obvious in the music room and the library. The servants kept fires in the rooms to dry them out. Two weeks later a messenger arrived announcing that the Fitzhughs were at Richmond and would arrive on Thursday.

"That's this afternoon," Lady Wilthrop spoke to Ellanor as they descended the stairs. "Depending on the roads, of course."

"It's been over two years," said Ellanor. "I wonder what they will think of me? I'm almost as nervous as the first time I met the Queen."

"I shouldn't worry, my dear. I'm sure all will go well." Lady Wilthrop nodded toward the stairs. "I think this carpeting will do."

"I remember the first morning I was here," said Ellanor. "I had never before seen carpeting on stairs."

"Do you like it?"

"I do. A nice change from the deep red."

Fines appeared. "The fires in the large sitting room have been built up, my lady. A light meal is ready at your pleasure."

The wait seemed endless, but within twenty minutes the coach arrived. Fines himself bowed Master and Mistress Fitzhugh through the door. Lady Wilthrop stepped forward to greet them and then stepped aside to allow Ellanor to greet her parents.

Master Fitzhugh took Ellanor's hand and bowed deeply over it. When he straightened, a smile covered his face. He kissed his daughter on each cheek. "My dear, you have become a beautiful lady." He stepped back, then quickly stepped forward again and hugged his daughter with absolutely no thought for the creases he left in her bodice and sleeves.

Ellanor's mother held out her arms to her daughter and folded her in a hug that lasted a long time. Mistress Fitzhugh finally stepped back and pressed her handkerchief to her eyes.

In the days that followed, Ellanor took her parents on tours of London and Westminster. They spent long hours exchanging news of Bishop's Manor and life at Court.

A week passed before Master Fitzhugh summoned Ellanor to Lady Wilthrop's parlor. After half an hour of earnest conversation, they emerged. Master Fitzhugh, his head bowed and his hands clasped behind his back, went into the garden. Ellanor slowly climbed the stairs toward her room.

The following morning Lady Wilthrop motioned Ellanor into her chambers. "I'm having a cup of tea. Come join me. Your parents are in the City today. Visiting the shops, I think."

Ellanor sank into a chair. "Thank you. I need a cup of tea. Entertaining guests is tiring."

The only sounds in Lady Wilthrop's chambers were the soft tink of spoons in tea cups and the low rumble of wagons in the Strand. A bright morning sun warmed the room.

Both women sat quietly enjoying their tea. Finally, Lady Wilthrop said, "I can't recall better weather in April. Quite unusual."

Ellanor nodded. "It's been perfect to see the sights."

"Your parents are pleased and impressed with your accomplishments. Your father comments frequently." Lady Wilthrop hesitated before continuing. "He spoke to me about his conversation with you."

Ellanor set her cup in its saucer. "It was rather difficult."

"Such conversations usually are."

"I don't believe that he was angry. He did, however, expect me to have a list of suitors ready to hand."

Lady Wilthrop nodded. "I'm sure he did. I promised him there would be."

"It's through no fault of yours, Lady Wilthrop. You've provided me with opportunities beyond all expectation." Ellanor set her cup and saucer aside and rubbed her forehead with her fingers. "I told him that I wish to find a man who is honorable and whom I respect. I told him that I want the same kind of marriage he and mother have."

"I'm sure that pleased him."

"I think it did, but I haven't yet found such a man. He must be disappointed. I know his heart is set on a title."

"He is worthy of a title," said Lady Wilthrop. "However, I believe he will not sacrifice you to an unsuitable marriage to gain one."

"No, I know that, but I wish I had met someone." Ellanor picked up her cup and saucer. "Would you like another?" She poured for herself and Lady Wilthrop.

"What about Lord Netherfield? You've become close friends with him."

"He is a fine man and a good friend, but he no longer needs to marry for money. He renews his fortunes with every investment. If only I could introduce Father to Lord Wetherby or even Lord Saxby. They prove that a title does not guarantee nobility of character or goodness of motive. Perhaps then—"

"You think if he knew them better—"

"—he might be less disappointed and a bit more patient."

Fines rapped lightly on the door. "Madam." He carried a small silver tray with a card on it. "A reply is requested."

"Please have the messenger go through to the kitchen to refresh himself."

Fines bowed himself from the room.

Lady Wilthrop read the card and gave an exasperated sigh. "Oh dear, oh dear." She shook the card as if to remove the name, the crest, and the message from it. "It's Lord Limbourne. He wishes to call!"

"To press his suit, no doubt," Ellanor smiled.

"He's beyond annoying. Of all the tiresome men . . . I wish he would admit defeat and retire from the field. So frivolous. Another good example for your father." Lady Wilthrop stared at the card. "My dear, an idea has come to me!"

"Sorry?"

"I believe we can show your father that all noblemen are not, well, noble. We'll give a dinner party with Lord Limbourne as guest!"

"My lady?"

"You must support me, however. I'm not sure I can last a whole evening in his company."

Ellanor gasped and then laughed. "You mean, use Lord Limbourne as an object lesson?"

"Can you think of one better? He's richer than the King—"

"He's completely self-absorbed." Ellanor said.

"He's ready to marry for greed, and best of all, he's an earl. I think he'll do nicely."

"Lady Wilthrop, I'd never ask you to do this for me."

"Perhaps your father will better understand what you have learned about the true value of a title, and I may find a way to end Lord Limbourne's attentions for good."

"We could invite other guests to help draw his attentions away from you."

Lady Wilthrop went to her desk. "Whom do you suggest?"

"It's been a week since Lady Esancy returned from Richmond. I'd like to introduce her to Mother and Father."

With a flourish of her pen, Lady Wilthrop requested the honor of Lord Limbourne's presence at supper the following Tuesday. She wrote a second invitation to Lady Esancy and added Lord Netherfield's name.

On Tuesday, promptly at seven o'clock, Lord Limbourne arrived. Master and Mistress Fitzhugh stood at the parlor window and watched his coach, drawn by four matched grays, pull up before Lady Wilthrop's door. Servants rushed to help his lordship alight. Fines announced his arrival and bowed him into the room where Lady Wilthrop and the Fitzhughs stood to welcome him.

Lord Limbourne crossed to Lady Wilthrop, took both of her hands in his, and kissed each of them. Then, knowing his condescension would please his hostess, he bowed gallantly before Ellanor and her parents.

Lord Limbourne had not spared his tailor in preparing for this evening. His deep green silk breeches were set off by a yellow brocade smallcoat worn under a pale blue brocade greatcoat. Lace fell in cascades at his throat and wrists. Gold rings, some set with precious stones, adorned his hands. His white silk stockings, embroidered with gold and silver threads, fitted his stocky legs perfectly. His shoes, a deep fawn color, were of the softest leather. He wore his hair after the current fashion, in long ringlets that bobbed whenever he moved his head.

Master Fitzhugh stood in astonished silence at the splendid form before him. He glanced down at his own sober attire. His dark gray greatcoat and breeches and plain white silk stockings that marked him as a prosperous and influential merchant faded beside the vision standing before him. A quick smile to his wife thanked her for insisting that he wear two gold rings and his lavender brocade smallcoat with a gold chain.

Master Fitzhugh was suddenly aware that Lord Limbourne was addressing him. "And how is the economy of the West Country? I've been to Bristol but, of course, I never dabble in commerce. My income is from my estates, which is as it should be considering my family's position at Court these last three generations."

Before Master Fitzhugh could pull his thoughts together to answer, Fines announced the arrival of Lady Esancy and Lord Netherfield and bowed them into the room.

Lady Wilthrop greeted her new guests and introduced them to the Fitzhughs.

Master Fitzhugh relaxed when he saw the sober good taste of Lord Netherfield's clothes.

Lord Limbourne greeted Lady Esancy with the respect due her degree and family. To Lord Netherfield, supporter of the Commons and secretary to Mr. Pym, he gave a quick nod.

Lord Netherfield gave a curt nod of his own.

Ellanor greeted the new arrivals. "Lady Esancy, I have missed your company this past month. Thank you for coming."

Lady Esancy responded with a kiss to each of Ellanor's cheeks.

Lord Netherfield bowed over her hand. He grinned and said, "Custom restrains me from following my Aunt's example."

Ellanor laughed and withdrew her hand. "My lord, comments will be made!"

CHAPTER TWENTY-NINE

QUESTIONS

After everyone was seated, Lord Limbourne picked up his conversation with Ellanor's father. "I have recently returned from York. I felt it my duty to attend His Majesty even though it was most inconvenient for me so to do. I fear he's abandoned Westminster and left Parliament in control of that rascal Pym. His Majesty will not return until Parliament submits to him."

Master Fitzhugh cleared his throat. "I beg your pardon, my lord. It's men like John Pym who guard the liberties of all Englishmen."

"Eh? I doubt that you know the truth of the matter living as far from the Court as you do."

Lord Netherfield stirred as if to speak. Lady Esancy's hand on his sleeve restrained him.

"I know as well as the next man what the King's taxes have done to families in the West Country. Some have mortgaged their very homes to be able to pay those taxes. Others have fled, leaving their land derelict. Only by a stroke of good fortune was I, personally, able to avoid paying a fine for refusing to take a knighthood."

"Ah, Master Fitzhugh," said Lord Netherfield. "I'm delighted to hear that someone managed to avoid that. I was not so fortunate."

Master Fitzhugh bowed to Lord Netherfield. "It was a shameless attempt by the King to push his hands deeper into our pockets. I commend Mr. Pym and his faction for ending that and so many other abuses."

Lady Wilthrop broke in to bid them to supper. Lord Limbourne immediately took his place as Lady Wilthrop's escort and led her into the dining room. The rest of the guests were left to organize themselves as they wished. Fines rolled his eyes when Ellanor passed him.

Mistress Fitzhugh squeezed her daughter's hand as they took their places. "Lord Limbourne has such an air of importance about him."

"Mother, Lord Limbourne takes advantage of every opportunity to impress Lady Wilthrop."

"Really? Is there a mutual regard?"

"No. He wishes only to add Lady Wilthrop's lands to his own."

"That man could become our neighbor?" Mistress Fitzhugh watched Lord Limbourne with greater care as she ate her soup.

"I say, Master Fitzhugh, your opinion is poorly stated and based on inadequate information." Lord Limbourne spoke with authority. "Now, if you had the confidence of the King, as I have—"

"Oh, dear," said Mistress Fitzhugh. Ellanor leaned toward her mother to better hear her. "Your father will be in a state tonight. He's not used to people discrediting his opinions. Though, I suppose, if Lord Limbourne speaks with the King—"

Lady Wilthrop broke in. "You've recently returned from Richmond, Lady Esancy?"

"Yes. It's early in the year to travel, but I long for the countryside from time to time. Richmond is beautiful in the early spring."

"We've lately arrived from the West Country," said Master Fitzhugh. "Given the state of the roads, I wonder that anyone travels at this time of year."

"We travelled on the Thames up and back. If the weather is nice, the journey is quite pleasant," said Lady Esancy.

Lord Netherfield turned to his aunt. "She has all the comforts. If it rains, we tie up at an inn. We are known at many of the fine inns along the river. It was a lovely journey."

"I would so enjoy a day on the river," Mistress Fitzhugh said to Lord Netherfield. "Would you give Master Fitzhugh the particulars?"

"Of course, before we take our leave this evening—"

Lord Limbourne interrupted the conversation by leaning over and whispering to Lady Wilthrop so everyone could hear. "You've heard, have you not, that the Queen has gone to Amsterdam? She took most of the crown jewels with her. Rumor has it that she will sell them to purchase arms for His Majesty."

"To fight against loyal Englishmen," said Lady Wilthrop. She continued, "I heard the Duchess of Richmond accompanied Her Majesty. I hope their crossing to Amsterdam was comfortable."

Lord Limbourne shook his head, sending his carefully arranged curls into flight around his ears. "I can't imagine they'll be happy among the Dutch." He turned to the rest of the company. "Her Majesty is so beautiful, so full of wit, while the Dutch are as dull as wet wood."

"The Dutch are a fine people, hardworking, good trading partners—"

Lord Limbourne continued as though Master Fitzhugh had never spoken. "Lords Goring and Arundel also took ship. Had you met them? Lady Carlisle didn't go, of course; the Queen wouldn't have a spy traveling with her."

"Isn't that overstated rumor?" asked Lady Esancy.

"Certainly not. Edm . . . Lord Wetherby has known for years of her spying. Why do you suppose she has suddenly retired to her country estate?"

"It is her custom to do so before the heat of the summer," said Lady Esancy.

"If Lord Wetherby suspected she was a spy, why did he not arrest her?" asked Lord Netherfield.

"He had no firm proof."

Lord Netherfield said, "I've never known that to stop him."

"You do him a great disservice. Lord Wetherby has always acted in the best interests of the realm."

"And himself."

"Are you referring to his appointment as Commander of the Guard? The King told me that he had to press, *press* his lordship, I say, to take the position."

"Is that so?" Lord Netherfield's tone let everyone know that he thought Lord Wetherby had needed no coaxing at all. "But, tell me, how did he propose to discover information against Lady Carlisle? Pray, tell, now that the Queen is abroad and the matter concluded."

Conversation lagged while soup bowls were removed and the next course served. As soon as Lady Wilthrop nodded the servants from the room, Lord Limbourne puffed out his cheeks and continued. "I happen to have been privy to Lord Wetherby's methods. From time to time he consulted with me."

Lady Wilthrop's knife hesitated over her roast beef. "He consulted with you?" she asked.

Lord Netherfield felt the light pressure of his aunt's hand on his sleeve.

"Indeed, and a most ingenious plan it was. You see, Lord Wetherby proposed to introduce spies into Lady Carlisle's household. He had two or three among the servants, though they did him little enough service for their pay."

Lilian, thought Ellanor. One of them had to be Lilian.

Lord Limbourne went on. "Unfortunately, the one from whom he expected the most, gave him the least, failing to report to his lordship even once. Most disappointing since his lordship went to great pains to place her. Now, he's set his investigation aside to attend the King in York. I advised him to stay and root out the spies against His Majesty. But he chose not to listen to me—"

"I shouldn't wonder—" said Ellanor's father under his breath.

It was Lady Wilthrop who continued the subject. "How could Lord Wetherby place spies in Lady Carlisle's household? Certainly, she would suspect—"

"It wasn't terribly difficult, actually." His lordship took a drink and wiped his lips before continuing. "We, Lord Wetherby and I, were chatting one day about Lady Carlisle. Simply as a matter of interest, I mentioned there was a vacancy in her ladyship's personal household. It wasn't two weeks later that he returned and said he had found someone to fill that position . . . to supply . . . information . . . Oh, my." Lord Limbourne glanced at Ellanor and then at his hostess. "Of course I had nothing to do with that. It was all Lord Wetherby's idea. As Commander of the Guard he . . . I . . . uh . . . ah . . ." Lord Limbourne took another drink.

"As I recall, it was you who told me of the wonderful opportunity awaiting my ward in the service of Lady Carlisle," Lady Wilthrop said.

Ellanor spoke softly, almost to herself. "He laid his plans over two years ago." She turned to Lady Wilthrop. "The meeting in the rose garden?"

Lady Wilthrop answered without taking her eyes from Lord Limbourne. "I believe so."

"My dear?" Ellanor's mother leaned toward her. "I've quite lost the thread of the conversation."

Lady Wilthrop studied the man sitting at her right hand. "Wetherby met Ellanor in Bath. It was you who encouraged me to place Ellanor with Lucy. I recall your distress when I said Ellanor was not ready for such a position. . . . To use her as a spy! Words fail me!"

"I know nothing! I repeat, nothing!" Lord Limbourne agitated his curls in denial. "As Lord Netherfield has said, the incident is over, and history is history. No harm done, eh?"

Lord Netherfield slowly folded his serviette and placed it beside his plate. His aunt's hand rested on his arm all the while. He placed his hand over his aunt's then turned to address Lord Limbourne. "In deference to the other guests and ladies now present, I'll refrain from expressing myself as I wish. However, my lord, I will call at your home tomorrow morning at my earliest pleasure."

Lady Wilthrop rang a small bell. When Fines appeared she spoke quietly to him. Then she addressed Lord Limbourne. "Your own words condemn you, my lord. It is best you retire."

"Re . . . retire, madam?"

"Your presence is no longer welcome."

"It was in service to the King. What could I have done?" Lord Limbourne held out a hand pleading with Lady Wilthrop.

Master Fitzhugh stood. He put both hands on the table and leaned towards Lord Limbourne. "Am I to understand that you were privy to a plan that endangered my daughter's life?" His words sounded like individual thunderclaps.

Lord Limbourne stood and pointed at Ellanor. "It was her own fault. Lord Wetherby couldn't get a word out of her about Lady Carlisle, or about Lord Netherfield, for that matter. That's why he threatened to ruin you—"

"Ruin me?"

Ellanor shuddered as she remembered Lord Wetherby's threats at the Guildhall.

Lord Netherfield rose from his chair. "I assure you, Limbourne, if any harm at all befalls this family, one horse goes lame, one brick falls from their chimney, that it is you who will be called up on charges by Parliament."

Lord Limbourne lifted his chin. "Come, now, Lord Netherfield. We are noble, men of breeding. She is a common wench with no knowledge of honor. She is as guilty of treason as Lady Carlisle for not serving her King."

Lord Netherfield spoke quietly. "Mistress Fitzhugh has great courage, character, and honor. You are a scoundrel, my lord, unworthy to utter her name."

Lady Wilthrop's voice dropped into the silence that followed. "Lord Limbourne, withdraw immediately from my home. I will never speak with you again, so I say now that in every possible way you have behaved abominably. Good bye."

Fines appeared in the entryway with Lord Limbourne's cloak, gloves, and hat. "Your coach is ready, my lord." He nodded to the two servants who had appeared behind his lordship's chair.

"Lady Wilthrop! Surely not! I have never been so meanly treated!"

The servants took his lordship's elbows and propelled him out the door.

Ellanor's mother took her hand. "Ellanor, dear, what is going on?"

"You need never worry that Lord Limbourne will be your neighbor, Mother."

CHAPTER THIRTY

FOR HAPPINESS

"Mistress Ellanor. Lady Wilthrop told me I'd find you in the garden."

"My lord, a pleasant surprise."

Lord Netherfield took Ellanor's hand and drew it through his arm. "Quite an evening, wasn't it?"

"Astounding. After you and Lady Esancy left, we talked until well after midnight."

"Your parents know the whole story?"

"Not all. Lady Wilthrop and I decided not to say anything about the river, at least, not for a few years. After Father's reaction last night, I think she's right."

"I'm happy I spoke with you first then. I might have said too much if I'd seen Master Fitzhugh first this morning."

"What will happen to Lord Limbourne?"

Lord Netherfield frowned. "He will continue as he always has, but he will always fear that his part in Lord Wetherby's scheme will become known. He'll be a quieter and, probably, a more circumspect man for a while."

They walked along the garden paths enjoying the warmth of the spring morning.

"You enjoy gardening?" he asked.

"I love the flowers, but I'm not certain about the actual planting and pruning. Lady Wilthrop has given me the privilege of planning the summer garden. Pity the gardener since I know so little."

They strolled to the fountain in the center of the garden and stopped to inspect the repairs to the stone work.

Lord Netherfield took a deep breath and let it out slowly. "Mistress Ellanor, we are friends, are we not?"

"Indeed, we are, these one and one-half years by solemn agreement."

"I must ask to change the terms of our agreement."

"You do not wish to end our friendship?" Ellanor asked.

"No, merely change the terms. Let me try to explain. Please, sit down. This might take some time."

He led Ellanor to a bench.

"When we first met, I was desperate for money."

"My lord, every man I met during my first winter in London was desperate for money."

"I had to pay taxes on my father's estates among other things. I confess, when I first met you, you represented pounds sterling and little else."

"You said you stopped thinking about Father's money. Besides, you now have made several successful investments."

"Let me finish. I've rehearsed this for quite some time, and I don't want to forget." He held up his hand to prevent any further comment. "When you visited Derbyshire at Christmas, I felt I wanted to know you better. But I didn't want any thought of money or marriage to cloud our friendship. Hence the agreement to be friends with no claims one on the other. Now, I need not put marriage off any longer. My family's fortunes are being slowly recovered." Lord Netherfield fell silent.

"Lord Netherfield, as your friend, I wish you happy. Have I the pleasure of knowing your future wife?"

"I believe so. Her breeding is most excellent; she is comfortable at Court and at private gatherings. Her company is much sought after by her friends."

"Goodness! Who is this wonderful person?"

"Again, you must let me finish."

"Sorry."

"She's loyal and puts the needs of her family and friends before her own, even to hazarding her reputation and life."

"This sounds like Lady Carlisle." Ellanor's eyes grew wide. "She's very beautiful as well."

Lord Netherfield leaned back and draped his arm over the back of the bench. He shook his head. "Not Lady Carlisle. She lacks a great deal in faithfulness. Come to find out, she really did provide information to Mr. Pym."

"That's impossible!" Ellanor faced her guest. "Then . . . then Lord Wetherby was right?"

"Surely you had an inkling."

"Never. I never guessed."

"Then I can add 'trusting' to my lady's list of attributes."

Ellanor frowned at Lord Netherfield. "I'm confused. However, I see why you must change our agreement."

Lord Netherfield clapped his hand to his brow. "Ellanor!"

"I beg your pardon?"

"*Mistress* Ellanor, can you not understand? I'm speaking of you."

Ellanor stared at the man sitting beside her. She opened her mouth as if to speak and then closed it. She felt as if the world had stopped turning but, somehow, she had kept moving. "Me?" she finally managed.

Lord Netherfield nodded.

The silence dragged on. Ellanor was vaguely aware of the warmth of the morning sun and the smell of the freshly turned earth. She heard herself say, "You've somewhat understated the matter."

"About?"

"About changing the terms of our agreement. This is no jest?"

"No."

Ellanor studied the fountain. Each of the repairs received her un-divided attention before she looked back at Lord Netherfield. "You've caught me quite unexpectedly. I don't know how to answer."

Lord Netherfield also studied the fountain before he turned to face Ellanor again. "I think I can finish my speech now with your permission."

Ellanor nodded.

"Mistress Ellanor, this has come as a surprise to me as well." He smiled at her. "Please don't take offense. I've enjoyed our friendship. With you I never had to be anything other than what I was, a poor nobleman. I tell you again that I almost never thought of your father's money."

Ellanor smiled.

"I always looked forward to our rides and conversations. You were the first I told of my investments. I knew you would listen without judgment. When I discovered your courage the night you came to warn Mr. Pym and his friends, I was amazed at your dedication and strength."

Ellanor felt herself blush. "To think that I almost became a spy without knowing it. I was so simple-minded. If Lord Wetherby had been a little kinder, I might have been more useful to him. You might now be in the Tower."

"I don't think so. You saw his meanness."

"Priscilla saw it first."

"I went to Richmond with Aunt Esancy to consider my growing regard for you. What I discovered was that I couldn't think of my future without you."

"I never thought—strange, but it was Priscilla who asked me about marrying you. Once you began to repair your fortunes, how-ever, I realized that you could marry anyone you wished. I never thought—"

"I'll throw all my profits in the Thames."

"That's hardly necessary and certainly foolish."

Lord Netherfield became suddenly serious. "Could you at least reconsider the terms of our agreement?"

"You will give me some time?"

"How long?"

"I don't know. I've always held you in high regard, my lord, but with no hope of being more than a friend. Our situations have altered so much these past months. Besides that, I am a Bristol merchant's daughter and must examine with care the terms of this new agreement you set before me."

"I await your decision."

"My lord, I still wish to marry for happiness."

Lord Netherfield smiled at the fountain. "I believe I shall."

"What's going on out there?" Master Fitzhugh joined his wife at the parlor window.

"I couldn't say, though they've been quite serious."

"Perhaps I'll go and find out."

His wife grabbed his elbow. "My dear husband, you'll do no such thing. See, even now they've come to some agreement."

In the garden, Ellanor and Lord Netherfield stood. She gave her best curtsy and he his deepest bow. They continued their walk in Lady Wilthrop's garden.